The Hollow Tree
Mystery

Tam
o' Shanter

The Hollow Tree
Mystery

MADELON ST. DENIS

COACHWHIP PUBLICATIONS
GREENVILLE, OHIO

The Author

Very little is known about the author, Madelon St. Denis. The use of 'St. Dennis' on her two traditionally published books appears to be a change by her publisher to accommodate marketing of those titles, as 'St. Denis' was often used on her magazine novels and foreign translations. 'St. Denis' is also how her name appears on a 1930 U.S. Census form, which notes she was born in 1885 in Massachusetts, and had been married at the age of 23. (She was 45 at the time of the census, lodging in New York.) One of her books, *The Death Kiss,* was made into a movie, so her name appears in conjunction with that in the 1930s, but she appears to have stopped writing by the end of the decade.

The Hollow Tree Mystery, by Madelon St. Denis
© 2024 Coachwhip Publications edition

First published June 1930, *Complete Detective Novel Magazine*
CoachwhipBooks.com

ISBN 1-61646-580-8
ISBN-13 978-1-61646-580-3

1

Paddy is Restless

"Tam—Tam o' Shanter!"

Molly's soft Irish voice rang across the sun-drenched yard, to lose itself in the green shadows of the orchard. Only the clucks of contentedly scratching biddies answered her and after a little she called again. This time a boy's tousled head was thrust out of the barn door.

"Whatcha want?" he inquired.

"There's a gentleman to see Miss Tam, on business he said. You know where she is?"

"Mebbe yes, mebbe no, 'pends on the kinda business," Dips hedged cautiously.

"Oh, it's a case, I'm thinking. He as good as said he wanted her help."

"Didn't say had anybody got murdered?" The boy's clever, freckled little face took on a distinctly hopeful look.

Molly considered before voicing an opinion. "The gentleman don't look to be het up enough for a murder. More like 'tis a robber he's needing help over."

"Even that's better'n loafin'. I'll go hunt her up." And Dips, small but efficient first lieutenant of the famous 'Tam o' Shanter, Inquirer,' departed with the speed of a lapwing, disappearing under the gnarled arches of the ancient apple orchard.

Quite regardless of the intense summer heat, Dips scud-
ded up the slope, making for a knoll from which could be
had an uninterrupted view of the clear-flowing Hudson.
He knew the spot as one of Tam's favorite retreats and
hoped that she might be there, awaiting the gorgeous pan-
orama of the approaching sunset. The small knoll gained,
he gazed eagerly about; but it seemed deserted, there was
no one in sight. Then, as he cudgeled his brain for some
alternative place to look, an accurately aimed and extremely hard green apple descended on his curly head.

"Ugh!" His surprised snort brought a teasing laugh
from the thick branches just above him.

"Nice detective you are!" Tam scoffed. "Aren't clues to
be found in the air as well as underfoot?"

She swung lightly from one branch to another, hung
for a second by her hands, then dropped to the ground beside him; a slender, khaki-clad figure looking much more
like a handsome, light-hearted boy than a clever pursuer
of criminals.

"Somebody wantin' you," Dips explained, staring at
her with his head cocked at an angle suggesting criticism.
"Mebbe I kin keep him jawin' whilst you change them
duds."

"What's wrong with these?" she demanded as they started back across the orchard. "Think I can't ask a stiff price
for my services if I look so unprofessionally youthful?"

"Looks like a boy's rig—nobody'd bank on you catchin'
no crooks," he grumbled.

But Tam only laughed at him, and, a few minutes later
introduced herself to the waiting viator without any
change of costume.

"You are the Miss O'Brien known as 'Tam o' Shanter,'
Inquirer?" he asked with a shade of incredulity in his
pleasant cultivated voice.

"Yes. Please don't feel discouraged by my present youthful appearance! I'm really quite a serious-minded person, professionally, which is what interests you, I imagine."

"As a matter of fact, I had expected to see an older woman," her caller apologized. "Your home was once pointed out to me by a former client and now, needing expert advice, I drove over to consult you."

After a little fumbling he produced a card neatly engraved with the name: "Simon Trevor, Cedarcliff, New York." Tam studied it thoughtfully, her interest really centering on the slight, distinguished looking owner of the unassuming card. He was a man well over sixty, almost effeminately gentle in voice and manner, yet with a hint of reserved power in his well-cut lips and steady dark eyes.

"Isn't Cedarcliff a village lying about halfway between here and the Sound?" she finally asked.

"A trifle more than halfway." She was later to learn that Mr. Trevor possessed a passion for exact statement. "We lie somewhat aside from the main arteries of travel, and I fear our village is rather sleepy and old-fashioned, indeed we're a conservative lot; which is probably the reason I've hesitated about starting any inquiry into my son's disappearance."

Metaphorically Tam's ears pricked with interest. At last he meant to state the reason for his visit! But she offered no comment, guessing that he could best unburden his mind if undisturbed by questions.

"After all, I may be unnecessarily anxious," he went on after a little reflective pause. "Three weeks is not such a long time, though it's certainly most unlike Lynn to leave me so long without news. My daughter-in-law feels that I am unduly troubled—that Lynn will return in his own good time."

"Have you any actual reason to think otherwise?"

"No definite reason, save that such an unexplained absence is most unlike my son, and— May I ask if you are fond of animals?"

Tam gasped at the apparently irrelevant question, but almost instantly realized it must have some bearing on his story, so she answered simply:

"Extremely."

"In that case you may understand the uneasiness caused me by the behavior of Lynn's favorite dog. Paddy, a most intelligent Irish setter, worships my son. Since his disappearance, the dog has behaved like one possessed by a demon of unrest. He refuses to eat, rambling constantly about the house and grounds in search of his master, and seeming to appeal to me for some help which I am unable to give."

"Hadn't you better start at the beginning and let me have the whole story?" Tam suggested. "You say your son has been gone three weeks—did he leave without any warning?"

"With absolutely none and in the middle of the night! As you say, I'd better acquaint you with all the facts. Three weeks ago, on the evening of July 7th to be exact, Lynn announced his intention of going down to the bank after dinner. I should perhaps, explain that Lynn is president of our village bank, a conservative, privately owned institution, and that at the time of which I speak his yearly vacation of one month was about to commence. Knowing this, his wife and I supposed him busy over some arrangements relative to the bank's running during his holiday, and were not uneasy when he failed to appear before bedtime. I, myself went to my room early, and retired a little before ten, but Ivy tells me she sat up reading until almost twelve, and he had still not returned."

"Yet you say his wife doesn't share your anxiety over his continued absence?"

"Not in the least. Indeed she's inclined to laugh at me."

"Do you know if he actually went to the bank?"

"Yes. The president's office has a private entrance, but Lynn forgot his key, so the night watchman admitted him."

"Does he know what time he left?"

"Not precisely. The door has a spring lock so it can be closed without a key. The watchman can only say that the office was empty when he went his rounds at midnight."

"Do you know if your son returned home that night?"

"He must have done so, though we none of us saw or heard him."

"Then how can you be sure?"

"Because his traveling bag is missing, also such clothes and toilet articles as he'd be likely to take if he intended being gone for a couple of weeks."

"One moment, Mr. Trevor. Do you mean your son returned home, calmly packed a bag and departed without leaving any note, or even saying good-bye to his wife?"

"That is what we presume to have occurred."

"Isn't it strange that his wife didn't wake?"

"Not particularly. He must have taken pains to be as quiet as possible and, besides, she wasn't sleeping in their bedroom, but on an adjoining porch."

"Such an abrupt departure without any leave-taking seems very strange," Tam commented. "Are you sure you're not withholding some of the facts?"

"No direct facts," he hastened to assure her.

"How about indirect ones? For instance, is your son's marriage happy?"

"Oh, ideally!" The old gentleman sounded distinctly shocked. "Ivy, his wife, is a charming, beautiful woman—they are devoted to one another."

"Yet he leaves, presumably for an absence of several weeks, without saying good-bye!"

"Well, the fact is, Ivy tells me they'd quarreled that day—a most unprecedented occurrence, I assure you."

"Oh!" The small word spoke volumes. "So they'd quarreled. Seriously?"

"I'm afraid so! Ivy believes that is the reason he suddenly decided to spend his holiday away from home, and that he'll return when the month is up."

"You don't altogether share her confidence?"

"To be frank, I don't. Lynn and I are particularly close—it's most unlike him to leave me without any word. After all, we had no quarrel. Also, as I told you, his dog's behavior alarms me."

"The dog hasn't acted in this way before, when his master was absent?"

"No, he generally mopes about the house, spending most of his time watching the front gate. This time he doesn't seem to be waiting for Lynn's return, he wanders in and out of the house and about the neighborhood, often whimpering in the most imploring way while he stares at me, or at Ivy."

"As if he was trying to tell you something, or to ask your help?"

"Exactly."

"You can't make out what he wants?"

"Not in the least."

Tam lapsed into a reflective silence, weighing the facts he had given and trying to decided their real significance. Was it simply the case of a piqued husband attempting to punish his wife, quite heedless of the anxiety the lesson might cost his innocent father, or did something more sinister lie behind the abrupt disappearance? It was difficult to decide from the scanty data at her disposal.

"You haven't consulted the local police, or made any inquiries?" Her long, blue-grey eyes regarded him with a certain friendly intentness, obviously missing no detail or expression or manner, and under their direct gaze Mr. Trevor moved uneasily, as if embarrassed by the situation or by his own part of querulously anxious parent.

"The police, no," he told her. "And I've questioned no one but the bank's night watchman."

"You've not spoken of a car. Does your son own one, and is it missing?"

"He had a roadster, yes, but it's still in the garage. We think he must have walked across country to one or other of the railway stations, and caught an early morning train."

"You just denied having made any outside inquiries," Tam reminded him. "Why are you so sure he didn't take a taxi to town, or to the nearest station?"

"The village boasts only a few cars for hire—if one of them had been used, I feel sure the fact would have reached my ears."

"Honestly, Mr. Trevor, I don't know whether or not to consider your anxiety justified. Suppose I drive over to Cedarcliff tomorrow and indulge in a little private inquiry? I should be able to advise you after personally going over the ground."

"That was my idea." He beamed approvingly. "In fact, it was to enlist your professional aid that I called today."

"Then suppose I report to you tomorrow morning, and refrain from putting any more questions now?"

"That would suit me perfectly were it not for one difficulty—my daughter-in-law."

"You think she would oppose an investigation into her husband's sudden disappearance?"

"Not if she entertained the faintest doubt that it was voluntary; but as it is, she's firmly convinced Lynn is only trying to punish her for their quarrel. She refuses to let me make any inquiries, declaring they'd render us both ridiculous."

"Then, unless you're prepared to override her objections, I don't see how I can help."

"I have thought of a way to avoid all friction." The old gentleman spoke with an air of decided pride. "Though my fear is that you may dislike playing an assumed role."

"Hardly. We detectives are used to discarding our own identities in favor of any role more suited to an investigation—I sometimes even change my sex, when a boyish part better fits the circumstances! What character do you suggest?"

"That of a trained nurse. While there is nothing seriously wrong, the doctors have pronounced my heart extremely weak; in fact, it was ostensibly for the purpose of visiting my physician in New York that I left Cedarcliff today. I planned, if fortunate enough to secure your services, to tell Ivy that my doctor declares the heart rather worst and advises a new treatment which can only be administered with the help of a resident nurse. In that way your presence in the house itself can be arranged without the slightest friction."

"It's quite a good idea," Tam admitted, thereby greatly increasing Mr. Trevor's liking for this businesslike but attractive young investigator of crime. "I can easily obtain a nurse's outfit, and unless I run across some doctor who'd be likely to spot the deception, I think I can successfully play the part."

At the word "doctor" he started slightly. Tam wondered why, but as he offered no comment she let the small mark of uneasiness slide. They arranged such prosaic details as the time of her arrival in Cedarcliff, and the fee to be charged for her work.

Just as Mr. Trevor, rose to depart, a second car joined the machine he had left parked before the house and Tam's father, ex-Chief of Detectives Rance O'Brien, climbed slowly down from the driver's seat. He was an immense man, both vertically and horizontally, fairly towering over slenderly-built Mr. Trevor. After a polite exchange of amenities the visitor drove away, while Tam and her father settled down on the broad veranda to watch the sunset; an almost nightly rite with them whenever they were in the country.

Molly brought out a tray laden with tiny warm cakes, for the creation of which she was famous throughout the countryside, and a frosty pitcher of fruit punch.

"Suppose that was a client—someone who'll be ending your holiday," Rance O'Brien grumbled as he sipped the cool drink. "Another murder?"

"Perhaps. At present it wears the guise of an unexplained disappearance." She proceeded to acquaint him with all the details given her by Mr. Trevor, then asked his opinion as to whether or not the son's disappearance was wholly voluntary,

"Not easy to say offhand. We'll need to know more of the personnel and setting. Ever been to Cedarcliff?"

"Only driven through. As I remember it's a lovely, old-world sort of place with one of the most delightful cemeteries I ever saw. Indeed, it was the beauty of its cemetery that impressed the name of the village on my mind."

"Don't happen to remember this bank he speaks of?"

"No. Of course you're wondering about its financial condition, and if any shortage of funds lies behind the sudden departure of its president."

"Naturally. That part will need looking into, once you're on the scene. Suppose you couldn't very well ask the man's own father if there was a chance of embezzlement."

"He'd have taken dire offense at the mere suggestion. Anyway the bank hardly seems the most promising angle— what interest me is his quarrel with his wife. I'm wondering what it was about and if there's anyone else involved."

"That's important," her father conceded. "All the same, you'll be wise not to neglect that bank. Unless my memory's going back on me there was some sort of banking scandal connected with Cedarcliff village just a couple of years back."

"You don't remember any details?"

"No, I've only a hazy recollection of something wrong there. Not an important case or I'd remember more about it. Why don't you phone headquarters and ask them to mail the particulars to you, at Cedarcliff?"

"I will." Tam smiled at him, a world of understanding love in her long, smoke-blue eyes. "That's one of the huge pulls I have over other private investigators—no one else has the best loved chief of detectives who ever retired from the force, as a father!"

"My old cronies do keep a warm spot in their hearts. But don't forget a lot of them have known and loved you since your toddling days. Believe they'd gladly go to as much trouble for you, as for me."

"And how it's helped in my work—that, and having you constantly ready to lend your advice!"

They lapsed into companionable silence, Tam nibbling a bit of cake as she stared at the blazing glories of the western sky while her father slowly filled and lighted that tried friend and counselor, an old well-seasoned pipe.

Next day Tam was duly met at the Cedarcliff station by Mr. Trevor, who regarded her conservative costume with an approving eye.

"You look the most demure and capable of nurses," he declared, leading the way to his car. "Shall I take the short cut home, or would you rather see the village?"

"Past your son's bank, if you don't mind; I'd like to see the exact position of his private office."

"It's not literally my son's bank," Mr. Trevor corrected her as they turned in the desired direction. "It's owned by a group composed of half a dozen men, Lynn being the only one among them who takes any active part in its management."

"If I'm to investigate your son's absence I'll have to ask all sorts of intimate questions, you know. So please don't mind my asking if the bank is prosperous."

"So far as I know, it's at present in good financial standing," Mr. Trevor assured her.

"'At present.' Does that mean it's been through a crisis at some past time?"

"Not quite that, but two years ago the cashier absconded with some of the bank's money and the report spread that he'd stolen much more than was actually the case. Something in the nature of a run on the bank ensued and for a few hours the situation looked serious, then the news that the absconder had been arrested and most of the funds recovered restored confidence. As a matter of fact he stole only a few thousand; the depositors' own panic constituted the only real danger. There's the bank now." He pointed an indicative finger toward a sturdy, ivy-grown brick building set a few feet back from the main street of the village. "Just glance down that lane to the left and you'll see a small projecting porch at the side of the building. The president's private office opens onto that."

Tam's trained eyes took in the necessary details, such as the extreme privacy of that small side entrance, as they drove slowly past. Leaving the village proper, the car turned into a wide, tree-bordered highway, flanked on one side by a row of secluded-looking houses, on the other by the cemetery, the beauty of which had impressed Tam on her former visit to the sleepy little village.

"Yes, we rather pride ourselves on the attractiveness of our graveyard," Mr. Trevor told her in answer to a comment on its beauty. "Indeed, my own house overlooks it and I've always congratulated myself on the fact, though some people might find such an outlook too mournful."

Here a fork in the road branched off from the main highway, and following the cemetery's edge, cut between it and the grounds of a large rambling house, their destination. The Trevor home actually faced the main highway, being set in the sharp V formed by it, and the side road they were following, but both drive and garage were close to the latter so that on leaving the car Tam and Mr. Trevor approached the house from the side and rounding the corner, came upon an effective tableau before their own presence was realized.

In the dappled sunlight and shadow of the wide veranda a slender, green-clad woman stood etched against the clinging masses of ivy, both hands pressed palm out against her eyes, as if to shut the blazing summer's day from her consciousness; while at her feet, in an attitude almost equally expressive of mental turmoil, crouched a large Irish setter, his silken coat exactly matching the dull auburn of the woman's soft hair. The color symphony of shadowy green and somber red so caught at Tam's love of the beautiful that she involuntarily stopped with a little pleased catching of her breath. Either this or the dog's instinct warned him of their nearness. He sprang up with one sharp bark, then, seeing Mr. Trevor, went to him, whimpering softly.

"What is it, dear?" The old gentleman touched the woman's shoulder almost caressingly, as her hands dropped and she stared at him half unseeingly.

"Nothing really—only a touch of the sun has made my head ache." With an effort she flung aside whatever thought had held her in thrall and smiled as brilliantly as though she owned not a care in the world.

"Not worrying about Lynn?" he persisted.

"Of course not! I'm perfectly certain he'll turn up once he thinks I'm sufficiently punished. But aren't you going to introduce us?"

Thus adjured, Mr. Trevor performed the necessary absent-minded mumbling of names winch generally does duty for formal introduction and the two women smiled at each other, a touch of instant camaraderie, in their eyes; women almost invariably like Tam on sight.

"I waited to welcome you, Miss O'Brien, before running off to keep an appointment. One of the maids will help if you need to make any special arrangements for father's new treatment."

"There, child, run along," Mr. Trevor broke in. "We'll manage perfectly. Are you going to the village?"

"No, only to see Linda; and father, you'd really better chain Paddy up! He's wearing himself out hunting for Lynn."

She pointed to the dog's anxious trotting back and forth—first to the veranda steps, then back to stare at Mr. Trevor, a troubled pleading in his soft brown eyes.

"Another instance of the innocent being punished along with the guilty." There was a caustic ring in Ivy Trevor's musical laugh. "Because I angered Lynn, he's allowing you and poor Paddy to suffer—rather a shame, don't you think?"

"Doubtless he doesn't quite realize."

"Of course not! Men never do." She turned and running lightly down the steps, disappeared around the house corner.

"I believe Ivy's begging to be worried, though she's too proud to admit the fact. Well, her absence gives us an undisturbed opportunity of searching Lynn's room for any possible clue."

"You don't seriously expect me to tell you where your son has gone, and why, just by the look of his room or the choice of articles made when he packed that bag? Remember I'm not a detective of fiction—I've no uncanny powers of intuition and I can't wring vital facts from a pinch of dust or three dropped hairs. Indeed my methods aren't a bit spectacular—they're largely painstaking observation, common sense, and a lot of hard work. Does that discourage you?"

"Not a particle! In fact, I find myself placing increasing confidence in your ability to get to the bottom of Lynn's strange absence."

"That's good news. To feel the people I'm working with are ready to trust me is almost half the battle. Shall we go in?"

"Perhaps I'd better first take Ivy's advice and tie up that dog—he's likely to make himself ill."

"Don't do that!" Tam narrowed eyes watched the Irish setter's hurried excursions down the steps, then back to Mr. Trevor; the same short journey repeated again and still again. "Has he been behaving exactly in this way ever since your son's departure?"

"Most of the time, though he now and then disappears for hours on end and comes back looking extremely dejected."

"I believe he's trying to lead you somewhere. See how he goes just a short distance, constantly looking back, then returns to you with that little whimpering cry— He's begging you to follow him!"

"Possibly you're right. Such an explanation hadn't occurred to me," Mr. Trevor admitted with the faintest touch of impatience. "But surely we can accept his guidance at some later time; it's more important to go over Lynn's room while the coast is clear."

"If you think so." Her tone held doubt, but she submitted to the postponement of any attempt to solve the puzzle of Paddy's conduct, and accompanied her host into the house.

2
Arsenic!

"And this is the porch where Mrs. Trevor slept?" Having finished a preliminary examination of the large, conventionally comfortable bedroom, Tam surveyed the adjoining sleeping porch with a slightly dubious air.

"Yes, she usually sleeps out here in the summer. Lynn prefers slumber within four walls."

"Do you know whether he entered by that outer door, or from the main part of the house?"

The younger Trevor's suite was situated in a wing on the ground floor, and her question referred to a door opening directly into the grounds.

"I scarcely know. Does it matter?"

"Only that it's hard to credit that an entry through the sleeping porch would not have disturbed Mrs. Trevor. Are the house doors locked at night, and had he a key?"

"Why no," her host admitted. "He usually rang if he was out late, or else entered through the porch. The front and side doors aren't locked during the daytime."

"Were any other keys used that last night? Any drawers unlocked to facilitate his packing?"

"Yes. A drawer in the highboy, where Lynn keeps certain personal papers, was open, so Ivy told me, and the papers tossed about as if he'd hurriedly searched through them."

"Any missing?"

"That I can't say. The drawer contains strictly private letters—we neither of us felt it necessary to examine them."

"It might be well to do so, though not quite yet. Were any other articles missing beside those he'd be likely to pack for a few weeks' absence?"

"Absolutely nothing."

Tam went back into the bedroom, where she commenced prowling slowly about, eyes searching ornaments and dresser furnishings as if in quest of some particular object. As a matter of fact she was only looking for anything unusual, any small item contradictory to the general scheme of things. Reaching the mantel she paused to regard it thoughtfully, then asked a question:

"Isn't that candlestick one of a pair?"

"Why, yes, they've been in the family for years."

"Then where's the other one?"

"I've no idea," Mr. Trevor admitted. "I think it belongs here on the mantel."

"Can you question one of the maids about its absence without causing comment?"

"It would be wiser to call Agnes in and question her quite openly. She's a dependable sort of person and never gossips."

He went to call her and Tam instantly dropped on her knees beside the half-filled wastebasket. A letter, torn twice across and badly crumpled, was retrieved and thrust into her handbag, also two crushed and partly faded roses. The remainder of the basket's contents failed to interest her and she was standing idly by the window when Mr. Trevor returned followed by a sedate, grey-haired maid-servant.

When questioned about the missing candlestick, Agnes declared that she had been unable to find it since the night of young Mr. Trevor's sudden departure.

"You're quite sure it was exactly at that time it disappeared?" Tam asked.

"Positive, Miss, because Mr. Lynn tossed his shirts and such all about in packing and I had to straighten them next day. That's why I remember the time for certain sure."

"Did you miss any other article, besides those he might be supposed to have taken with him, on that particular morning?"

"I did, Miss—the black cat used for a door-stop was gone."

"Nothing else?"

"Nothing at all, except what Mr. Lynn put into his bag."

"Thanks. That's all I wanted to ask."

Mr. Trevor dismissed the maid with a caution against repeating the conversation to anyone, then turned eagerly to Tam.

"Do these missing objects give you any clue?"

"A suggestion, at least. Shall we take up my role of trained nurse, now? Your daughter will think it queer if I'm still in street clothes when she returns."

Swallowing his unsatisfied curiosity, Mr. Trevor led the way to the room on the second floor prepared for her use. It was just across the hall from his own, within easy calling distance. As Tam unpacked her bag and changed into a crisp white uniform, her mind dwelt rather sadly on the coming sorrow which she feared was about to overshadow the life of her kind old host. Long association with crime and the suffering it caused so many innocent victims, was never able to destroy her warm Irish pity for those of her clients who were crushed beneath undeserved trouble—a weakness, perhaps, yet at the same time a strength, for it lent her an understanding sympathy that won confidence and trust from those about her.

Descending to the lower floor, she found Mr. Trevor just opening the front door to a visitor, a fluffy, gushing little lady, well past her first youth. She had greeted him with an enthusiasm that seemed faintly embarrassing to her dignified host, who hailed Tam's advent with quite obvious relief. He hastened to introduce his new nurse to Miss Linda Clyde, then asked Miss Clyde what had become of Ivy.

"Why, I haven't seen her today! Was she looking for me?"

"I understood her to say she was going to your house."

"Oh, really! Then I'll rush home! She must have arrived after I left. Goodbye, dear Mr. Trevor—so glad to have met you, nurse." And she departed amid a cloud of over-strong perfume and over-abundant chiffons.

"Our nearest neighbour," Mr. Trevor explained in a slightly resigned tone. "She owns that yellow house you probably noticed as we drove up the lane; the one just behind this."

"I remember it. There's nothing more we can do in the house at present. Shall we follow Paddy's guidance?"

"Certainly, if you really think he wants to lead me somewhere."

But the Irish setter was no longer in sight when they went out on the veranda. Nor did he answer to repeated calls, so they were forced again to postpone learning what it was which, as Tam believed, the dog longed to show his master.

She glanced at her wristwatch, then declared her intention of strolling through the cemetery before luncheon time.

"I think clearly while walking alone," she half apologized for declining his offer to accompany her, "and already there are one or two things that need thinking about."

It was a rocky, cedar-crowned cliff in this same cemetery which gave the village its name, and the precipitous little ravine that ran at the cliff's foot quickly drew Tam by the sound of its shallow, merrily chuckling brook. She picked a way down to the water's edge and there perched on a moss-grown rock, lighted a cigarette and gave herself to consideration of Lynn Trevor's disappearance.

Was it voluntary, or the result of foul play? She leaned increasingly toward the latter supposition, yet there were other facts which contradicted it, chief among them his wife's attitude. That she was worried, possibly unhappy, seemed fairly obvious; her pose when Tam first had seen her against the ivy background of the veranda was far from that of a happily contented woman, and her eyes also had told of some concealed trouble or anxiety, though there had been nothing in look or manner to suggest intense fear or grief—it seemed, rather, as if she perhaps knew the reason behind her husband's abrupt departure and possibly shared the secret of his present whereabouts; a supposition rather strengthened by her own story of having slept through his return and hurried packing. Tam had no faith in that avowed peaceful slumber in close proximity to a man in the throes of selecting and packing the necessaries for an absence of several weeks.

Had Lynn Trevor really consulted his wife, confided to her the facts which made a sudden absence imperative, and cautioned her against telling anyone, even his own father?

If that were true, it seemed that some discreditable motive must have prompted a departure so sudden as almost to savor of flight.

On the other hand, why were those two dissimilar articles missing? Dissimilar, yet sharing one common quality, a quality which hinted at a certain sinister reason for their absence. The mate of the missing candlestick was very heavy, tall and formed of massive bronze; while doorstops, too, were usually weighty affairs. What better articles could be chosen on short notice for the effectual sinking of, say, a packed bag which it was necessary should never again see the light of day?

Tam sighed impatiently, flung aside her cigarette and lighted another, for again that puzzlingly undisturbed slumber of the missing man's wife cropped up to confuse her train of thought.

If, just conceivably, some stranger had passed through the sleeping-porch, entered the bedroom and, unfamiliar as he must have been with the exact location of the desired clothing, had yet so successfully packed and carried off one of Lynn Trevor's bags that the selection of the articles taken had aroused no suspicion in the minds of those who best knew Lynn's wardrobe—still, how was it possible for Ivy to have slept tranquilly through the whole proceeding? If, that is, she had actually been sleeping on the porch at the time, as she had stated!'

Well, that was one of the questions that needed looking into. And another was where that same lady had been during this present forenoon. After openly announcing her intention of calling on Linda Clyde, she had quite obviously gone somewhere else—for the two houses, while not very close together, were much too near for the two women to have missed one another on the way. Besides, Ivy had been gone for at least an hour when Miss Clyde had called at the Trevor house and denied having seen her friend all morning.

Again, why had the two yellow roses found in Ivy's wastebasket been so viciously crushed and thrown there? They could not have been flowers left by her husband, for they were only slightly faded; and he had been gone more than three weeks. As for the letter rescued from the same receptacle, it was only a somewhat cryptic epistle suggesting an appointment for golf and signed simply "Rodney," in a sprawling, careless sort of script.

Last, but by no means least, why was Lynn's favorite setter so determined on leading Mr. Trevor to some unknown spot? For that such was the dog's desire, Tam entertained not the faintest doubt. What did Paddy know? What sinister scene hod those soft brown eyes looked upon? She was aware of a decided regret for having permitted her host to overrule her suggestion of following Paddy at once wherever he wished to lead. Well, perhaps the dog had returned to the house by now—better go back and see.

She jumped up and, skirting the unclimbable cliff, attained a higher level, then followed a shady bypath which she guessed ran in the desired direction. A little further along she heard voices, then came upon two workmen, or rather gardeners, who were performing an almost surgical operation on the trunk of a stately tree. Its dead wood had been cut away, the inner bark scraped, and now the men were filling the wound with partly-cooled tar.

Tam paused to watch them. Her policy when on a case always included friendly gossip with any chance-met strangers on, or near, the scene of her investigation; one never knew what stray bits of unlooked-for information might thus be collected. In this particular instance there was nothing of interest forthcoming, however; she merely learned that the men were employed by the Government Forestry Commission, with whom some special arrangement had been made by the Cedarcliff City Council relative to the overhauling and doctoring of the cemetery trees and shrubs.

Just inside the gate by which she had first entered, Tam's always watchful eyes were attracted by a sudden glitter at the extreme edge of the path. It was gone almost before noted, yet her habit of investigating trifles caused her to search for the object which had for a brief second caught and reflected the noonday sun.

She was rewarded far beyond her rather vague expectations; a huge, particularly beautiful opal lay half buried in the grass.

It lacked any setting, having apparently fallen from some piece of jewelry; and its position, well settled into

the earth with several blades of grass sprawled across it,
suggested that it had lain there for some weeks. She admir-
ingly examined the stone, then slipped it into her purse,
meaning to at once tell Mr. Trevor of her treasure-trove.

Tam had been absent from the house longer than she
realized. She found her host rather anxiously watching for
her, but before she could mention the opal the luncheon
bell rang and they went into the dining room, where Ivy
Trevor joined them. Something warned Tam against speaking of the opal in her presence, and so she waited a later
opportunity of showing it to Mr. Trevor.

During the meal, Lynn's absence was not mentioned. It
was only when they had finished and were indulging in
friendly cigarettes, that anything connected with Tam's
secret investigation occurred. Then a faint scratching
sound came at the side door which opened directly into
the dining room. Ivy said: "That's Paddy! He wants to
remind us that luncheon tidbits are much appreciated by
even the best trained of dogs."

With the words, Ivy rose and went to open the door.

Slowly, painfully, the big Irish setter crawled across its
threshold and collapsed, piteously moaning, at her feet.

Instantly Ivy was on her knees, the dog's head lifted to
her lap while she crooned over him, stroking the wide red
forehead with tender fingers.

"Paddy, dear old Paddy! Has he made himself sick hunting for Lynn?" she murmured. "The sun's too strong, old
boy, much too strong!"

"It's not the sun!" Tam had risen and now stood looking down at the suffering animal. "The dog's been poisoned! Arsenic, I think—is there any doctor near whom
you can send for?"

"Poisoned!" Both her hearers echoed on a note of con-
sternation.

"Impossible!" Ivy sounded sharply horrified. "No one could want to kill Paddy! He's the best natured dog alive! Everybody loves him!"

"Nevertheless, if you want to save him you'd better got a doctor at once," Tam retorted.

"Oh, how awful! Father, please phone to Rodney! He's apt to be in now."

The two girls did what they could to case the dog's suffering, and in a scant ten minutes the doctor for whom Mr. Trevor had telephoned, arrived. Tam liked his gentle though skillful handling of the canine patient, and in her character of nurse, helped him to administer a dose of hot mustard-water, later followed by raw eggs beaten up in milk—wondering, the while, if it was the close proximity of this doctor, who could not possibly had reached the house so quickly unless he lived close by, which had caused Mr. Trevor's slightly guilty start when she had mentioned the risk of a doctor's trained eyes promptly piercing her assumed role.

"Can you save him, Rod?" Ivy Trevor asked when Paddy had been carried to an improvised bed in the rear hall and seemed somewhat relieved of pain.

"I think so. He's always been healthy and the arsenic wasn't down long enough to get in its full work. Any idea where he got it?"

"Not the least! It's inconceivable that anyone should purposely poison him, yet where could he have picked it up?"

"He couldn't—or at least it's hardly possible; arsenic's not a thing generally left lying about." The doctor again stooped over the dog then straightened, eyeing Tam with a certain curiosity, "Thanks for your help, Nurse—"

He left the sentence m the air, an open request for her name; which Ivy supplied.

"Nurse O'Brien. I told you father is trying a now treatment for his heart and she's to be with us, I hope, for some time."

"To make the introduction complete, you might add that I'm the rising young practitioner of this neighborhood, name of Rodney Poole—whose practice at present consists mainly of playing veterinary to all the animals owned by my friends; they won't yet trust me with human patients."

"Absurd!" Ivy laughed at his aggrieved air. "Simply because Daphne wanted you to overhaul her prize chickens, and now we've sent for you about Paddy!"

"*And* Linda Clyde's pet cat, and her parrot, to say nothing of that unspeakable little beast she calls a marmoset," he checked off the items on supple brown fingers, his dark eyes dancing with amusement.

"Oh well, Linda—" Ivy's tone spoke volumes and Tam, having glimpsed the lady, guessed she was just the type to keep innumerable pets and inflict their ailments on her friends.

"I think we should go into some other room and let the dog sleep," Mr. Trevor here advised.

Accordingly all four adjourned to the cool, wide-windowed living room, where Tam displayed a professional interest in seeing her patient comfortably settled, then announced her intention of walking down to the village drug store to buy a few things necessary for the new treatment. Rodney Poole promptly suggested driving her down, but she declined the offer, saying the walk would do her good.

Following Ivy's careful instructions, Tam cut through the cemetery and a small wood just behind it, so reaching the village without touching the main highway. Her first visit was to the Western Union, where she sent off a discreetly worded message to her father, requesting him to drive Dips over to Cedarcliff next day, and appointing a place of meeting. That attended to, she strolled slowly up the main street, presently entering the village's one modern drug store. Quite a well-equipped affair, it had not so far progressed as to boast a luncheonette counter, but there were numerous small tables at which its patrons might be served with soda or ice-cream, and many of them were occupied.

Tam bought one or two things at the drug counter, then sat down at one of the tables, ordering an ice-cream soda. As she slowly enjoyed it, she lent an attentive ear to the scraps of conversation that reached her from nearby tables. One could never tell what enlightening bit of gossip might not thus be picked up, free of effort.

For the first few minutes, her present attempt to listen in on conversations not strictly meant for her ears seemed to promise scanty results, but patience is one of the qualities most needed by a detective. And when a youngish, extremely good-looking man—whose presence caused an obvious flutter among the group of women at the next table—entered and went to the soda-fountain, almost the first comment caught strengthened Tam's faith in the help so often given by unsuspecting gossipers.

"Mighty perky Bob's getting, now Lynn Trevor's away!" one of the women remarked. "You'll remember he never showed his nose, after coming out of prison, so long as Lynn was about."

"They always did dislike each other, them two," a bespectacled matron contributed with a nod of reminiscent wisdom. "'Twas only Lawyer North ever got Bob Payne into the bank."

"And a sorry day for them all when he done it! Running off with the bank's money like he did, and going to prison and all."

So—the young man pleasantly chatting with the soda clerk was the absconding cashier of whom Tam had heard! Luck was certainly with her.

"I did hear as Bob swore, along the time of the trial, that he'd sure get even with Lynn Trevor once he come out," a quiet little woman who had not hitherto spoken, volunteered. "Seems like he blamed him for not hushing things up out of court, once the money was give back."

"Oh, it never ended there!" The first speaker, refusing to be outdone, drew her listeners closer with one comprehensive glance, then related some choice morsel of news in a voice so low that Tam could catch no more than an occasional word or phrase: "Went to him right in the president's office—after prison—Sheriff Ferguson says— Oh, a terrible scene, terrible!—Bob Payne went and pulled a gun—"

"Shish—sh—" The smallest woman hissed in a sibilant whisper that carried far more distinctly than an ordinary tone of voice. "There's his sister, Patience! She looks like she knew we was talking about Bob!"

Instantly the small group fell to discussing the latest church news and market prices so audibly as to leave no doubt in any one's mind as to the entire innocence of their conversation, and Tam turned to look at the sister whose entrance had so abruptly ended their little feast of scandal.

She was a tall, badly-dressed woman, whose wretchedly cut frock was tight in all the wrong places, giving her figure a quaint, irregularly bulging effect in no wise redeemed by the oily, carelessly arranged black hair and muddy brown skin; a commonplace, not to say dowdy, person, who in no way resembled her handsome brother at the soda fountain.

Idly Tam watched as the woman clumped flat-footedly across the store, spoke to her brother Bob Payne, then went out again without having bought anything. She rather hoped that her gossiping neighbors might take up the trail once she was gone, but they only paid their modest reckoning and went out, on example she decided to follow.

Out on the street again, Tam loitered past the bank, and casually explored the lane upon which its side entrance opened. Then, as the afternoon was fairly well along and she imagined that the bank watchman she wanted to interview could only be seen at night, she started back toward the Trevor house.

Tea was being served on the veranda and, contrary to the procedure in more formal houses, Ivy Trevor at once invited her father's nurse to join them—she evidently meant treating Tam quite as one of the family.

Young Dr. Poole was still there, and the group had been augmented by Linda Clyde and the doctor's sister, Daphne—a really lovely girl whose coloring, softly pink and white and yellow, suggested some delightful French confection, too fragile to be energetically touched, even by a caress.

"And how did you like our village, Miss O'Brien?" Daphne Poole asked when Tam had been supplied with a cup of fragrant tea.

"Liking is almost too mild a word! I've quite fallen in love with the place—particularly the cemetery."

"Everybody does. Of course the cemetery is our real beauty-spot and lover's retreat; still, it's rather a slur on our civic pride to hear people admire it so much more than our attempts at modern progress."

"So sorry, but I never noticed any," Tam laughingly admitted. "I thought their absence one of the village's chief attractions."

"Never say that to any member of our council!" Daphne implored with mock horror. "They'd never forgive your not having noticed our brand-new library, in a remodeled cottage, of course, and our even brander-new post office, building and all."

"Stop making nurse believe we're all moss-grown old fogies!" Ivy Trevor scolded her friend. "She'll start getting as bored as Patience North looks—than which no attitude of mind could be more dismal."

"Oh, Patience!" Linda Clyde sat up, with an interested flutter of numerous scarfs. "I hear that Jasper North refuses to have Bob Payne in the house, and for once his long-suffering wife asserted herself—she always was devoted to her scamp of a brother. They say there was a battle royal and the Norths are hardly on speaking terms."

"Trust Linda to collect any scandalous reports floating about!" Rodney Poole's tone betrayed more than a touch of irritation. "Hasn't poor Mrs. North suffered enough on Bob's account? Now that he's paid for his fault and is out of prison, why not try to forget the whole unfortunate affair?"

"That's easy to say," Linda retorted. "But how can one forget when Bob hasn't the good taste to live somewhere else, but insists on hanging about Cedarcliff, where we can't help but see him!"

"Give the poor devil a little time! He's only been free a few weeks; naturally he clings to his sister just at first."

"Oh, if you're sure that's the reason he stays!" Linda snapped. "Personally I've heard whispers of quite a different reason."

"You would!" Rodney jumped impatiently to his feet. "Come on, Ivy, let's you and I have a look at our patient."

They went into the house together, and the subject of Bob Payne's continued presence in the village was dropped; much to Tam's regret.

3
The Missing Opal

"Hum-m, does look fishy—nobody'd steal a bronze candle-stick and a door-stop for their value."

"Of course not. That's why I want Dips to explore the countryside and report all likely places where a weighted bag could be sunk without much danger of its ever being found."

The three had met at the designated spot, well outside Cedarcliff village, and leaving Rance O'Brien's car parked by the roadside, retired into a little wood for private confab. Dips, who had been listening with much the expression of an alert terrier, here put in a question:

"Wells get included?"

"I'm afraid so, particularly if they're not much used. But specialize on any ponds or deep brooks—the one running through the cemetery is too shallow, as far as I've followed it."

"Want I should stay in the village?"

"Yes. Pose as a gardener's assistant out of work—I'll arrange with Mr. Trevor to have his man take you on."

"Pretty well decided there's been foul play?" her father asked, and Tam thoughtfully considered the question before answering it.

"Why else were that candlestick and door-stop taken? If only one were missing, we might conceivably think up a plausible reason, say affection for an old heirloom in the case of the candlestick, or liking for the little black iron cat designed as a door-slop—some of them have a really winning smile! But when two such heavy articles are stolen, it's pretty certain they were taken only for their weight. Lynn Trevor would hardly want to sink his own bag and go off minus even a razor. It's much more reasonable to suppose someone else packed that bag and disposed of it, meaning to create the impression that Lynn had left of his own accord."

"Puzzling, though, how a stranger could have done the job without rousing Mrs. Trevor—unless she was drugged."

"That would spell premeditation, and also rather narrow the number of possible suspects." Tam spoke with reflective slowness. "As far as I can learn, she was only in touch with Mr. Trevor, the Pooles and Linda Clyde during that afternoon and evening; they seem the only ones who had an opportunity to drug her. No, I don't think drugged sleep is the answer we're looking for."

"Too bad you didn't follow the dog while you had the chance."

"Yes! Stupid of me to neglect that obvious lead. His poisoning, and so soon after I got here at that, seems the most sinister happening that's occurred so far. It suggests a murderer who'd read Paddy's actions just as I did, and hastened to put him out of the way as soon as any suspicious stranger appeared on the scene."

"Could the murderer, supposing there is one, have recognized you?"

"I suppose so, especially if it was someone who'd been in Sing Sing—you know my work takes me there fairly often."

"Meaning this lately released absconder, I suppose?"

"Well, you'll admit Paddy received that dose of arsenic suspiciously soon after my advent. Of course it was meant

to kill him, but we acted so quickly that I think he'll re-
cover—it's only question of days before he's able to show
us whatever he's been trying to reveal to Mr. Trevor."

"And you think that will prove—?"

Tam only grinned at him, refusing to rise to the bait,
then turned to Dips:

"Besides hunting a possible watery grave for Lynn's
bag, I want you to learn all you can about Bob Payne. Get
a line on his general habits, disposition, friends, and if
it's at all possible find out where he was the night Lynn
Trevor disappeared. That last won't be easy; very few people ever remember what they were doing on a given date,
three weeks previously—but have a good try. Oh—" She
repeated the scraps of talk overheard in the drug store,
adding: "If possible, make friends with the village sheriff,
Ferguson is the name, I think—I'd like to know if Payne
made any definite threats against Lynn Trevor."

"I suppose there's no way I can help?" her father inquired on a rather wistful note.

"Not at present, dad-dear, except digest the case and
get ready to disgorge helpful advice when I run into some
sort of hopeless snarl—as I probably shall a bit later on."

After a little more talk they separated and Tam walked back
to the Trevor house. Neither Mr. Trevor nor his daughter-
in-law were in evidence; indeed, the lower floor seemed
deserted, until a low-toned muttering drew Tam into
the living room, to find the maid, Agnes, on her knees,
violently scrubbing at the rug with some particularly
evil-smelling gasoline. It was her muttered complaints
against the stubbornness of spots in general, and the inef-
ficiency of that gasoline in particular, which had reached
Tam's listening ears.

"Makes it look worse, so it does!" The maid glanced
up as she sensed the approach of a possibly sympathetic

watcher. "Who'd ever think a bit of tar would stick that bad?"

"Tar? Are you sure it isn't a piece of chewing gum? How could tar get in here on the rug?"

"That's what I asked myself the day I found them spots of it about the house!" Agnes sat comfortably back on her heels, dramatically waving the gasoline rag, much pleased at a chance of airing her troubles. "But tar it was, Miss— once I'd scraped it up with a knife there was no mistaking the smell—and since then I've tried soap and water and I don't know what all, trying to get out the stains, but sure it's there for keeps!"

"Perhaps it had set too long—when did you find it?" Tam put the question idly, quite unprepared for the maid's answer.

"The morning after Mr. Lynn up and left us! Sure, Paddy was out of doors that night, though most generally he sleeps in the house, and 'twas him tracked in the tar."

"What makes you think so?"

"It's not thinking I am, Miss, but knowing! I'd me doubts if the dog wasn't to blame, so I looked at the feet of him and sure enough, the front two had gobs of tar stuck to his toes."

"That's curious. I wonder how it came there?"

"Who'd ever be knowing where a dog gets the dirt he do be tracking about a house?" And with a protesting sniff, Agnes returned to her rather futile scrubbing at the spot on the rug.

Tam watched her, wondering what connection, if any, the tar on Paddy's feet bore to his master's disappearance; had he followed Lynn along some path or road that had been freshly tarred? Too bad so much time had elapsed! It might be difficult, now, to learn exactly where tar had been used on the day previous to Lynn Trevor's disappearance.

Her next question was put with an air of innocence that might have deceived a far more suspicious person than Agnes:

"Is Mr. Trevor expected back soon? His wife must be lonely without him."

"Oh, she's not the lonely kind, Miss, being too friendly with everyone for that—though she do seem mighty fond of Mr. Lynn, I'll say that for her."

"I'm glad of that; it's nice to know such a beautiful woman is happily married. What's he like?"

"Oh, a fine figure of a man, Miss, not overly tall, but that well set up and spruce—All the girls do be looking after him."

"They must be a nice couple to work for."

"That they are, never did I work in a house I liked better."

Just then the front door bell interrupted their friendly chat and Tam offered to answer it so as not to drag Agnes from her enemy, the spot. It was the postman with a registered package, for which Tam was about to sign when Ivy Trevor flashed down the stairs and almost snatched the small package from her hands.

"It's for me!" Her voice held a quite unnecessary sharpness. She signed the registry receipt, then turned and vanished up the stairs almost as rapidly as she had descended them.

Tam looked after her reflectively. Without Ivy's obvious annoyance over the incident, the precise shape and appearance of the registered article might not have so impressed themselves on her mind. As it was she found her interest very much aroused; and made a careful mental note of the size and shape of the disturbing little package, which, she was sure, bore the name and address of a well-known New York jeweler, and unless she was much mistaken, contained the sort of box generally used to hold a ring.

Why on earth should its advent so upset young Mrs. Trevor?

Tam wandered out to the veranda, settled herself in one of its comfortable wicker chairs, then puffed a meditative cigarette as she thought over the case, not so much trying to foresee its next development, as carefully to weigh the facts already known.

If Lynn Trevor had been murdered, as she now felt was increasingly probable, there seemed one person at whom the finger of suspicion strongly pointed—young Robert Payne. According to the overheard gossip he, at the time of his trial, had blamed Lynn Trevor for his imprisonment. Was he the sort of man to harbor a grudge and exact blood vengeance after the lapse of two years? Also was he familiar enough with the internal arrangements of the Trevor house, and the habits of its occupants, to have been capable of packing that deceptive bag, and—equally important question—did Paddy consider him a friend, so that he would not have raised an alarm had he seen Payne entering his master's room? Though, and here Tam gave herself a little mental shake, it was far from certain that the dog had been close to the house at the time it was entered by whoever packed that bag. Agnes stated he had been out-of-doors during the night in question; it was quite possible that some private canine business, such as a battle or a courtship, had taken him away from home at the critical hour. But in that case, why was he so anxious to lead Mr. Trevor to some unguessed destination? Surely the dog knew something concerning the events of that night! Well, in a few days he'd probably be enough recovered to guide them—in the meantime she must possess her soul in patience, and try to prove her theory that the missing bag had been sunk in some convenient stream or pool.

Here Ivy Trevor put an end to Tam's meditations by coming out of the house, as serenely smiling and friendly

as if she possessed not the faintest rudiments of the temper which Tam had glimpsed less than a half hour ago.

"I suppose I don't need to tell you father's lying down,"
she remarked, accepting a cigarette from Tam's offered
case. "As his nurse you probably know what he's doing
better than I do."

"I'm afraid not in this particular instance," Tam admitted. "After our morning treatment I indulged in a solitary
walk, and had only just returned when we met in the hall."

Ivy ignored the veiled reference to her impatient seiz-
ing of the registered package, and turned the subject to
her father's health.

"Don't think me rude, Miss O'Brien, if I confess your
presence makes me terribly anxious; his heart trouble must
have taken a really serious turn, to make the doctor think
a resident nurse necessary."

"Truly, it's not so much that, though of course his heart
is anything but strong," Tam explained, feeling herself a
most conscienceless deceiver, "as that he believes under
proper treatment the old trouble may be lessened. Do you
know enough of anatomy to understand a technical explanation of the case?"

"Heavens, no!" Ivy hastily denied. "Please don't try
offering me anything of that sort, I'd listen without the
faintest conception of what you were talking about and
afterwards feel convinced such long words meant father's
case was nearly hopeless."

Tam, who would have been much embarrassed had her
offer been accepted, smiled with the touch of superior
wisdom proper to a trained nurse.

"Medical terms are apt to sound rather appalling, if one
isn't accustomed to them! But honestly I don't think you
need worry especially about Mr. Trevor's condition, though
I do think he'd be much better if only he could rid himself
of some anxiety that seems to be preying on his mind."

"Of course he would! That's why it's so fiendishly self-ish of my husband to have left his father without any word, simply because he wanted to punish me!" Ivy responded with a flash of the temper that evidently slept not too deeply beneath the lovely tranquility of her outward self. "Well, he's been gone a trifle over three weeks, and his holiday from the bank only lasts for a month—we can expect him back next week. And then, believe me, the quarrel which sent him off will fade into insignificance when compared to the piece of my mind I intend giving him!"

And her deep, sun-flecked brown eyes blazed in a way that left no doubt as to just how frankly she would deliver the aforesaid fraction of her mind.

"You don't think Mr. Trevor's anxiety about his son justified, then?" Tam risked betrayal of a slightly suspicious knowledge for the sake of learning Ivy's reaction.

"Not the least bit in the world, as I've told him all along," came the instant answer. "Lynn was simply furious with me, and after our quarrel went down to the bank and brooded over how he could get even—hitting on the happy thought of a mysterious disappearance, he proceeded to carry it into effect that same night! And with the selfishness of all men, never gave his father's suffering a thought. I only wish he knew how little his absence has worried me! Oh, here comes Rodney."

Young Dr. Poole called a good morning from the side lawn, then joined them, disposing his long, lazily supple length with the air of one on familiar ground and sure of welcome.

"Drifted over to see my patient—how is the old chap?"

"Apparently doing nicely," Ivy informed him. "Though I must say you're a neglectful physician. Here it's almost lunchtime, and you never even called up to inquire how Paddy felt."

"I was sure two such nurses could attend to him," Rodney defended himself. "Besides, Linda's marmoset overate, at breakfast, and had an attack of colly wobbles—I've been holding his paw for the past hour, while his fair mistress whispered soft nothings into my ear!"

"Since when has Linda taken to wasting her blandishments on you? I thought she reserved them all for father's benefit?"

"Oh, she does—it was about him the soft whispers revolved. I say, Ivy, if you don't watch out you'll be having our dear Linda as a mother-in-law."

"Not while father remains conscious!" Ivy retorted. "He can't abide her; literally flees on sight."

"Much good that'll do him! It takes a mighty clever man to avoid matrimony, once a woman really makes up her mind to marry him. Well, when it happens, don't say I didn't warn you! Ah, here enters the intended victim."

He rose as Mr. Trevor emerged from the house, pulling forward a big chair and generally seeing to the old gentleman's comfort in a way that still further won Tam's liking; she had scant patience with the casual treatment accorded the older generation by most modern youth. For a time the conversation was general and touched on nothing that particularly interested Tam, then, as Ivy's slender hand was outstretched to fleck the ash from her cigarette, her father-in-law said pleasedly:

"I'm glad to see you wearing your opal again, Ivy. You know I admire that ring, and have missed it lately—in fact, I rather feared something had happened to it."

"Happened to it?" Ivy echoed almost sharply. "What put such a notion into your head? I've worn it quite as often as usual; you simply haven't noticed."

"No." Mr. Trevor shook a gently stubborn negative. "I'm especially fond of opals and I haven't seen yours since—let me see—" Here his passion for exactitude sent his mind back in search of the precise time. "Not since Lynn's last dinner with us."

"That's really absurd!" Ivy sounded distinctly annoyed. "I'm certain I've worn it since then; there's been nothing wrong with the ring and no earthly reason why I shouldn't wear it." Then, with a sudden change of tone: "If you like the opal so much, father, let me have it made into a scarf-pin for you—I'd love doing it."

"Thanks, my dear, that's like your generosity, but I'd far rather see it ornamenting your little white finger."

Thereafter no more was said concerning the opal, and Tam lent an only half attentive ear to their talk. The whole episode of Ivy's ring, taken together with the unset opal which she herself had found on the cemetery path, so intrigued her curiosity that she found herself questing an explanation. Mr. Trevor, with his care for the precise statement of any fact, would scarcely declare she had not worn it since the night of Lynn's disappearance unless he was very positive of the fact; but if such was the case, why her vehement denial, why her insistence that she had been wearing the opal right along?

Had she actually lost the stone from its setting on the night in question and later had it replaced by another, which had only arrived by registered post that morning? Such an explanation fitted the facts—but why such secrecy?

Her obvious anger when Tam had started to sign for the registered package, the almost equal irritation betrayed at Mr. Trevor's mention of the ring, suggested some more serious reason than a mere reluctance to acknowledge having lost a valuable stone—if, of course, the opal found by Tam was really the jewel originally belonging in Ivy's ring. Was it possible that Ivy feared having lost it in some place where she was not known to have been, during that particular night? Here Tam reined in her thoughts. She was taking far too much for granted; better not let her mind run off at a tangent until more facts came to light.

All the rest of that day passed pleasantly enough, but with nothing accomplished. Tam rather chafed under the feeling that she was simply marking time, and the arrival on the last post of a long, plain envelope from headquarters, containing the official reports of Robert Payne's trial, was a distinct relief. As soon as possible after dinner was over, she went up to her own room for a careful study of the reported case.

After a year's honest though not specially brilliant service at the Cedarcliff bank, young Payne had suddenly disappeared and a shortage of several thousand was discovered in his books. Inquiry showed that he had recently been gambling and losing rather heavily, also that the sums taken spread over a period of several weeks. He had been arrested in Boston after a short but strenuous chase, and part of the missing money recovered. The remainder his brother-in-law, Jasper North, had offered to make good, at the same time begging that the case might be dropped without further criminal proceedings since it was Bob's first offense.

All the bank directors save Lynn Trevor had declared themselves willing to rest content with the regained money. But Trevor, the bank president, had held out for trial and sentence, insisting that an example be made of young Payne. Lynn had won—Bob was duly tried and sentenced to two years at hard labor.

So that was the reason behind the released prisoner's animosity against his former chief! Tam wondered just how deeply his sense of grievance had cut, just how much it had been brooded over during the long months in Sing Sing.

Here she moved impatiently.

Heavens, what a noise the crickets and katydids were making! It was almost impossible to think.

Then, as she listened to the insistent chorus, a certain oddity in the notes of one particular insect caught her attention. Surely a giant of its species, to judge by the loudness of its voice! It persistently departed from the recognized formula—"Katy-did—Katy-didn't," to repeat over and over "Did—did—did."

Tam laughed softly to herself, locked away the report from headquarters, and tip-toed quietly from her room. She strongly suspected human design behind that unconventional "Did—did—did!"

Gaining a side door without meeting anyone, she slipped out into the grounds, heading away from the house and, crossing the lane, entered the cemetery, sure that her white nurse's uniform would act as a guide to Dips if he had really been signaling her.

"Mighty deaf some 'uns gets, once they stick a nose to paper," her small assistant grumbled as he silently joined her just inside the cemetery gate. "Seen you camped by that winder, and near wore out me pipes tryin' to call you 'ithout letting on to the whole darned family."

"You've something special to report?"

"Yep. I got it!" his tone vainly struggled to conceal his triumph.

"Not Lynn's bag?"

"Sure! What else was. we lookin' arter—less'n' it was the corpse!"

"Where?"

"In a pond, a piece down the road from here."

"Tell me." Tam sat down on a convenient tombstone and the boy crouched beside her, pouring out his story in short, eager whispers.

"First off I hunted deep water like you told me. There ain't none, 'ceptin' wells—all the brooks hereabouts is that shallow you couldn't sink more 'n a matchbox. 'Bout 'steen million wells—I figured 'twould need all hot weather to sound 'em—then I come on this pond, not so deep, but fairish and sizable, looked the best bet I cud spot."

"It's near here?"

"'Bout a quarter mile down the highway—headin' away from the village."

"And?"

"I'd seen a big bunch o' kids playin' ball whilst I snooped round—hunted 'em up arter I'd spotted the pond, got chummy and showed 'em some wrinkles 'ith a bat—we all got het up, like I knew we would, so I sung out for a swim. Fine, we trailed down to me pond, offn' our clothes and duv in. Arter a bit I played to find a big clasp-knife o' mine, down to the pond bottom—got 'em all wantin' to know what else 'ud be sunk an' divin' to find out. One kid, minister's son, hit on the bag stuck a'tween two rocks—too heavy fer one! So three on us duv an' brung it up, then I let on 'twas serious—stopped 'em from openin' it and we all swore on shut mouths. Minister's kid helped me hide it, an' I waited 'til dark to wise you."

"Splendid, Dips!" Tam warmly approved. "It was much wiser to get help from those boys than to start an official search before we were sure the bag was there. Did you have time to hunt up the sheriff?"

"Yep. Got a line on him from 'em kids—nice friendly gink an' easy to steer. Palled up to him later, lettin' on I was out o' work—seems a jolly sort 'ithout much spine."

"Do you know if we can reach him tonight?"

"Thought o' that!" Self-satisfaction rang loud in the boy's voice. "He'll be down to the Inn, over checkers, 'till round eleven."

"Then we'll hunt him up—I'd sooner not alarm Mr. Trevor until we're certain the recovered bag really be-longed to his son, yet I don't want to open it without a police witness. If the bag proves the one we think, we'll need official help in searching for the body. I don't mean that finding Lynn Trevor's bag actually proves he's been murdered, but it greatly strengthens the supposition that he didn't voluntarily leave home."

"Good bit of woods and such, but it's an openish country—queer nobody's stumbled acrost the body, effin 'twas lef' lyin' round loose." Dips had evidently already accepted the certainty of Lynn's death, and was only hopefully concerned in the finding of his body.

"It is strange," Tam admitted. "If it's near here, it must be pretty effectually hidden; buried, perhaps."

"Hit me it mightn't be bad to set them kids on the hunt," Dips offered. "Youngsters most and generally knows more about woods and sech than grownups. Whatcha think?"

"I think that, subject to the sheriff's consent, we'd better put your pack of boys on the trail first thing tomorrow morning."

4
Red Ants

Somewhat water-dulled but still perfectly legible under
the flaring gas-jet of Sheriff Dan Ferguson's office, the
two letters stared up at the small group of curious humans
as if dumbly imploring justice.

Dragged, by Dips, from his nightly game of checkers,
the sheriff had listened to Tam's version of the case and
her own connection with it with a most absorbed interest, afterwards accompanying Dips and the famous young
woman investigator—whom he insisted on regarding with
a kind of astonished awe—to the place where the former
had hidden the rescued bag.

"The lock's so rusted we'll have to force it," Tam began, adding: "No, it may prove important later, to know
if the bag was locked with its own key; we'd better cut the
leather."

"You're sure it's all right to open it with only us here?"
the sheriff anxiously inquired. "Oughtn't we let Mr. Trev-
or know?"

"Not yet. I want to spare him as much as possible, and
besides, I'm working for him, while you represent the police."

"Reckon as you know best."

Under her directions he cut a long gash parallel to the
bag's locked frame, then two lesser cuts which allowed

the side to be dropped down like a flap. Just inside, with curled pink tongue and plaintive green eyes, sat the little black cat designed as a door-stop.

The sight of the grotesque little animal practically removed Tam's last doubt, but to make assurance doubly sure they partly explored the bag's contents. Shirts, underwear, ties, socks, and toward the bottom some sort of light woolen suit; all were crammed in with such utter disregard of any attempt at packing as convincingly to prove that whoever filled that bag never had expected to wear any of the garments included; their mashed condition would have rendered them entirely unfit for use, even had they not been water-soaked.

"Guess it's Lynn's, all right." Ferguson was the first to speak. "What do we do next?"

She told him of Dip's idea that the village boys should be organized for a systematic search of the countryside, adding:

"That part I'll leave to you, as I want my name kept out. I can work much better if people don't know I'm a detective."

"Don't believe we kin keep folks from catching on to what we're after," Sheriff Ferguson declared. "Still, they're that used to seeing boy-scouts clipping over the country, they won't take particular notice just at first. Maybe by the time they've woke up, we'll have located Lynn's body. You think his bag being sunk in the pond shows he's dead?"

"At least it gives us definite enough suspicion to justify thorough search."

"Mightn't the body have been took off somewhere in a car?"

"Surely, only in that case why leave the bag so near home? It's reasonable to suppose it was packed as a blind, after the murder—unless, of course, the whole thing was a carefully planned, premeditated crime, in which case we've no guide as to the sequence of events. It's best to work our way, one step at a time—and the first is to try and satisfy ourselves as to whether or not Lynn Trevor's body is concealed anywhere in this vicinity." She eyed the water-sodden bag reflectively, then asked: "Is it true that Bob Payne made threats against young Mr. Trevor's life?"

"If you call barging into Lynn's office and pulling a gun on him making threats, he sure did! You know about that bank trouble, a couple of years back?" Tam merely nodded and he went on. "First week Bob came out of prison he kept pretty much under cover—kind of dug himself in, in that shack he has a ways back from the cemetery wood. Nobody saw him, excepting his sister, and they do say her and Lawyer North had trouble over his going to their house. Then one night some of his old pals went up to the shack to kind of welcome him back—must have took a good bit of booze along and made a night of it, because next morning Bob showed up at the bank with an awful hang-over, forced his way into Lynn's office and threatened to shoot him.

"Lynn and one of the tellers jumped on him and there was a free-for-all. Bob sobered up enough to apologize and swear good behavior if Lynn'd overlook what happened— so they dropped it at that. Bob kept clean out of sight until he knew Lynn was gone away, then he started being seen around the village just like nothing had ever gone wrong with him."

"He'll bear close watching—now."

"You—you don't think—" Ferguson stammered.

"I'm not giving an opinion at present—but revenge is sometimes a powerful motive. Are you the only peace officer in the village?"

"Yes, what would we need of more?"

"Then you'd better swear in a trustworthy deputy before the search starts tomorrow, and have him keep an

eye on young Payne. We don't want him vanishing to parts
unknown before we learn something of his whereabouts on
the night Lynn disappeared."

While her advice seemed a good deal of a shock, Ferguson agreed to follow it, and they separated on the understanding that he was to attend to securing a deputy, and
later join Dips at his arranged meeting place with the village youngsters.

On entering the Trevor house Tam found her host waiting for her—a rather embarrassing habit of his, which she
felt must later be cured somehow. Seeing no necessity for
wrecking his night's rest, she told him nothing of the recovered bag, only explaining that she had been busy making certain inquiries in the village.

It was only after he had breakfasted next morning that
she finally told the old gentleman her news. He took it so
bravely that Tam felt his suspicions must all along have
been more serious than he had admitted, even to her; and
she liked the way in which, the first shock over, he metaphorically squared his shoulder, and faced the probable
issue.

"Dan Ferguson is not the man to successfully handle
any important case," he impartially asserted. "He's quite a
good sort, honest and painstaking, but he lacks brains. If
these boys fail—"

He paused a second, a hand covering his eyes, then
went on with a certain proud courage. "In that event we
shall need official help. Will it be possible to go over Dan's
head to State or City police?"

"The former is more usual," Tam told him. "But if I run
into town myself and use a bit of Irish blarney at headquarters, I think the Homicide Bureau will agree to make
a special arrangement with the State Constabulary so that
one of their own inspectors can be detailed on the case."

"You'll go in today?"

"Immediately, and later phone the sheriff from head-quarters to learn if there's any news. Is there a convenient train?"

"In a half hour. I'll drive you to the station."

"Thanks, I can change in ten minutes."

She was as good as her word, taking her place in the wait-ing car long before he had really begun to expect her.

"If you don't mind the suggestion, I think you should tell Mrs. Trevor that her husband's bag has been found," she told him during the drive to the station. "The news is almost sure to leak out and she might hear it from some outsider. Only please don't enlighten her about me. I can work best if I stick to the role of your trained nurse."

He promised to prepare Ivy for whatever event might develop, and left her at the station, seemingly surprisingly little shaken by the partial confirmation of his worst fears regarding his son.

At headquarters, Tam quite shamelessly used her influ-ence to upset the machinery of the usual police procedure, so well succeeding that she was even able to have her old friend and colleague, Inspector Peter McCoy, put on the case. After Tam had telephoned to Sheriff Ferguson, learn-ing that so far the impromptu search had been barren of result, the two put their heads together, mapping out a tentative plan of action.

Tam then caught an afternoon train back to Cedarcliff, arriving in good time for dinner. It was a rather doleful meal. Mr. Trevor ate in almost complete silence, apparent-ly deep in thought, while Ivy seemed dazed and more than a trifle inclined to be snappy. It was a relief when Rodney Poole and his sister dropped in as coffee was served.

"Ivy has been shamefully neglecting me all day," the lovely Daphne complained as she deposited a butterfly kiss on Ivy's cheek. "Simply forced to come over and see if anything was wrong—besides, your cook makes such delicious coffee."

"So that's the reason you rushed me away from an only half-finished dessert!" her brother reproached her. "Shameless little glutton! And I thought it was anxiety about Ivy, not a hankering after her coffee, that put you in such a fidget!"

Daphne pointed the tip of a rose-pink tongue at him otherwise scorning a reply, then gratefully accepting a cup of fragrant coffee at the hands of their host. Tam left them, talking about nothing in particular, and went out to the cemetery and Dips' report.

It proved purely negative. His posse of youngsters had scoured all the most likely places they could think of, but had discovered no sign of a hidden body—no indication of any newly made, unauthorized grave.

Indeed, when not only that first day's search, but the second and third, earned out under the experienced supervision of Inspector McCoy, proved equally fruitless, it began to seem that their conclusions were wrong, and either no crime had been committed or the body had been taken elsewhere.

Tam still clung to her belief that Lynn Trevor had actually been murdered, and his body concealed somewhere in the vicinity, but both McCoy and Sheriff Ferguson were inclined to skepticism and frankly admitted a reluctance to pursue the search. Better wait, they said, until the four weeks of Lynn's holiday were over and see if he turned up, or at least until the dog, Paddy, so far recovered as to be able to lead them to whatever spot he had tried to draw Mr. Trevor to, before he was poisoned.

On the fourth day after the discovery of the sunken bag, Tam, returning from a counsel in the sheriff's office, took the short cut through the cemetery and, tempted by the peaceful beauty of the shady, velvet-grassed place, stopped to rest and think.

Was the missing Lynn Trevor cheerfully enjoying his holiday without the faintest suspicion that his dead body was being searched for at Cedarcliff? No, she refused to believe herself altogether mistaken. What earthly motive could he have had, in the first place, for packing a bag in so untidy a manner that only a trained valet's service could make its contents usable, and in the second, sinking said bag in a lonely pond? Nor could the latter act have been merely the result of sudden impulse; the inclusion of candlestick and black cat proved intention. Moreover, why should some unknown person have poisoned Paddy on the very day Tam took up the inquiry into Lynn's disappearance, if there was nothing to hide?

"Oh, damn!" In her absorption, she had thrust out one foot, failing to notice that the movement placed her ankle in close proximity to a ribbon of hurrying little red ants. Her exclamation was caused by their emphatic disapproval.

Astonishing how viciously such tiny things could bite! And what an army of them! Tam leaned down to watch the purposeful march of the countless throng, each hurrying unit so bent on performing its own appointed task.

Idly following the moving stream, seeking their objective, she saw the head of one column disappearing into the tiny crack of a nearby tree, while a second column emerged half an inch lower down. The tree which was absorbing their attention, a gnarled old oak, was evidently one on which the men from the Government Forestry Commission had exercised their skill; for one whole side of the trunk was faced with tar, as she had seen them filling in the decayed hollow of another tree on the day of her arrival in Cedarcliff. This was a much larger tree, however, and the cavity treated must have penetrated deep into its

ancient heart, for the tar-filled wound in the trunk commenced a good five feet above the ground, widening to a
breadth of more than two feet as it neared the bottom.

It was into a slight opening left between tar and bark
that the ribbon of ants was vanishing. Rather odd, Tam
thought—knowing, as a country dweller, that these small,
determined pests were decidedly carnivorous in their
tastes, with a depraved preference for any meat left unpro-
tected by a careless housewife.

Meat! She jerked suddenly erect, then went closer to
the oak tree, her eager eyes on the marching ranks of the
red army.

What was tempting them into its heart?

The upper part of the tar facing was evenly smoothed.
But lower down, especially at a height of a few inches
from the ground, it was deeply scored by irregular vertical
scratches, dozens of them, of varying length and depth.

Into Tam's long eyes leapt the dancing green flame that,
with her, spelled discovery of some vital clue, or the birth
of some new idea.

Like a flash she was off toward the village, running
through the cemetery and the Church woods with the easy
speed of trained muscles and a perfectly conditioned body.

Inspector McCoy and the sheriff, peacefully discussing
the case amid a cloud of tobacco smoke, were startled almost past speech as the usually self-contained Tam dashed
in upon them and without a word of explanation, demanded the instant procuring of a couple of pickaxes.

"Oh, I'll explain on the way!" she impatiently shut off
McCoy's half-uttered question. "Only don't waste time
talking— Get two pick-axes!"

A hasty trip to the village hardware store supplied the
required implements, and the two men joined Tam in the
Church wood, where she was waiting for them, not wanting to be seen in the village in their official company.

"I may be wrong," she told them, leading the way into the cemetery, "but I believe Lynn Trevor's body is entombed in a doctored oak tree! You've got to open it up and make sure."

Momentarily ignoring their stream of questions, she only answered them when the tree was reached. "You see the red ants? They're after some food inside the tree trunk—and those deep scratches in the tar—don't they suggest the work of a dog's paws, frantically trying to reach his master?"

"Paddy?"

"He tracked tar into the house—this may be where it came from! And finding himself unable to get at Lynn's body, he tried to secure Mr. Trevor's help."

They fell to vehement attack on the hardened tar, which crumbled easily enough under the bite of a pickaxe, since it was not designed to withstand more violent usage than that of wind and weather. Starting fairly well down, so as to run as little risk as possible of injuring the body they believed the tar to encase, they worked at first rapidly, then with increasing caution.

Presently they uncovered a section of partially charred newspapers Then, using the pickaxe with the utmost care, they removed the tar bit by bit, until—

The unmistakable outline of a human body wrapped in newspapers and roughly tied, was revealed standing upright in the hollow heart of the tree!

The tar, necessarily applied to the cavity while hot, had badly charred the papers. But when they were at last able to lift out the freed body and, laying it full length on the grass, cut off its enclosing envelope, it was found to be surprisingly little injured by its almost month-long entombment. The nearly complete lack of air and the action of the slightly bituminous tar had so well preserved it that there was not the slightest doubt as to its identification; it was Lynn Trevor who lay before them—murdered.

Guided by the red ants' trail, they vehemently attacked the hardened
tar in the gnarled old oak-tree. The outline of a human body, wrapped
in newspapers and roughly tied, was revealed standing upright within
its hollow trunk

The latter fact was unquestionably established by the wound just over his heart. It was a knife-wound. The knife itself had been withdrawn. A clean cut through the left coat-breast showed where it had entered and the flesh which McCoy promptly uncovered, revealed the corresponding deep stab.

"M—m— Not so much blood, considering the knife was pulled out," the Inspector muttered. "May have died instantly, in which case the flow would be a bit less, or may be the knife was left in until after circulation had stopped. Damned clever way of hiding the body— Nobody but Tam would ever have found it!"

"More good luck than good work," Tam reproached herself. "I should have thought of it without the help of those ants! But I never had sense enough to really look at that tree until they practically pointed it out."

"You translated their parade and the dog scratches quick enough, though." McCoy grinned at her approvingly. "Next—what do we do with the body? Has this village got a coroner?"

"Sure!" Ferguson sounded indignant at the mere suggestion of any official lack in Cedarcliff. "Rodney Poole's our man. Not that he's ever served as coroner, there ain't been any need, but he got appointed a year or two back. I'll go fetch him."

He cut off toward the Poole house, which stood on the edge of the cemetery remote from the village.

"Better have a go at his pockets." McCoy knelt beside the body, his skilled fingers investigating the clothes for any possible clue; only the usual contents of a man's pockets such as keys, purse, matches and the like rewarded him until he reached the left trouser pocket.

Folded small and tucked into its furthest depth was a small scented note, or rather the upper portion of one:

"Dearest:—Love— Tonight at ten, caref—"

"So—" Tam's eyes met McCoy's with a flicker of half-amused surprise in their grey-blue depths. "Despite vivid accounts of the young Trevors' devotion—enter another lady! That note wasn't written by his wife, for I've seen samples of her hand and it's utterly dissimilar."

"Puts a different face on the whole affair," the Inspector grumbled, "and a bit weakens suspicion against Bob Payne."

"Not necessarily! The fair unknown may be some sweetheart of his—may even furnish a *double* motive on his part."

"That's possible," McCoy rather dubiously admitted as, his initial examination of the body finished, he spread one of the less charred newspapers over the dead face. "This paper, dated the seventh of July, pretty well establishes the time of the murder—couldn't have been earlier because he was alive on that date, though of course it might have happened later on and the papers been a day or two old when used."

"So probable that he was kept prisoner somewhere and later butchered in cold blood!" Tam sarcastically retorted. "In your place, I'd stop hunting round for more trouble until after I'd questioned Bob Payne as to his whereabouts on the night of the seventh."

"Oh, I'll do that fast enough—if he hasn't a watertight alibi he gets popped into jail."

"Still, if he's really guilty he's sure to have fixed up some sort of alibi; they always do. Here come the sheriff and Dr. Poole."

The sight of his friend's body plainly affected Rodney in no uncertain manner. His handsome, generally irresponsible young face was haggard, drawn with shocked horror.

"Poor old Lynn!" he muttered, kneeling reverently to remove the newspaper with which McCoy had covered the dead face. "Who'd have dreamed he'd meet such an end? Does his wife know?"

"Not yet," it was Tam who answered. "We thought it wiser to have you present when they're told."

"Why?" he shot out the question, straightening to stare at her.

"Not so much for her sake as for Mr. Trevor's," she explained. "You see his heart's weak, a physician may be needed."

"I see. Very wise of you, Nurse."

Did she imagine if—or was there the faintest possible stress on that last word, "nurse?"

His strong, supple fingers moved here and there over the body, pressing the flesh near the wound, lifting the closed eyelid.

"If one of you will go to the village and arrange for some sort of stretcher, we'll take him to the undertaker's. I can't perform an autopsy at the Trevor house and there's no other place."

"I'll go," the obliging sheriff offered, perhaps prompted by a fear of being left to guard the body alone.

"Very well." Rodney rose and for a second stood silently regarding the body of his friend, his features twisting with an emotion that rather astonished Tam—who, while liking him, had hitherto not given him credit for much depth of feeling. Then his shoulders jerked back as if flinging off some unwelcome weight, and he turned to face McCoy. "You'll stand guard here, Inspector, until the men from the village arrive?" The two men had previously met, so that he already knew McCoy's police rank. "Nurse O'Brien is perfectly right; I'd best be on hand when the old gentleman is told."

They might, however, have spared their anxiety. Mr. Trevor took the news of his son's murder like the thoroughbred that he was—a momentary flinching, a deathlike pallor that told of strain on the weakened heart, that was all.

But with Ivy it was different. She quite frankly went to pieces and indulged in violent hysterics, which took the efforts of both doctor and nurse to finally subdue.

"To think we quarreled on our last day together!" she sobbed piteously, collapsing into a moist, crumpled heap in Tam's arms. "And now he's dead—dead—so I can't ever tell him I'm sorry!"

As her plaintive self-reproachful wail died under a storm of frantic weeping, Tam happened to glance up and into a nearby mirror. What she saw there caught at her breath, for a second stopping it as effectually as a jolt of ice-water.

5

A Girl's Logic

"I'll admit drawing a gun on Lynn Trevor—but that doesn't mean I killed him!"

Young Payne, very erect, very defiant, eyed the assembled group with unveiled hostility.

They were gathered in the Trevor living room, Mr. Trevor having offered the house as McCoy's headquarters since the sheriff's office was much too small and inconvenient for prolonged use. Not actually under arrest, Bob was being questioned as to his exact doings on the night of the murder, and was finding the process anything but pleasant.

"You'll also admit considering Lynn Trevor responsible for your years of prison and having, at the time of your trial, threatened to get even once your term was served?" McCoy persisted.

"Am I allowed to advised my client as to the wisdom of answering possibly incriminating questions?" The speaker, Jasper North, was present because of Bob's insistent claim that he was entitled to a lawyer's help and advice.

"He's already been warned that anything he says may be used as evidence against him," McCoy grumbled with a resentful side glance at the lawyer's impassive mask of a face. "If he's innocent, frankness is by all odds his best bet."

"Oh, I'm innocent fast enough, but it's damned hard to prove just where you were on a given night, nearly a month ago."

"At the moment we're dealing with a time still further back," the inspector reminded him. "Did you, or did you not, utter threats against Lynn Trevor's life at the time of your trial?"

"I may have," Bob sullenly admitted. "A man's apt to say more than he really means when he's as sore as I was then. You see, if it hadn't been for the president's veto the directors would have let me off without criminal proceedings after Jasper had made good the money loss. Can't much blame me for bearing him a grudge."

"What I want to know is just how deep that grudge went, and if you nursed it along while in Sing Sing."

"Well, I guess I didn't altogether forget it."

"And you came out ready to put your former threats into effect?"

"That I don't admit. Maybe I hated Lynn Trevor, but I didn't go after him or hunt any trouble, except that once when I was half-seas over after a night with the boys."

"You deny harboring any intention of paying back the wrong you felt he'd done you?"

"I meant to let sleeping dogs lie. Besides, what could I do? Look at the chasm between his position and mine—then you'll see I was helpless."

"Unless you meant taking his life as payment."

"I tell you I'd no such thought!" Bob fairly shouted at the dapper little Inspector, whose insistent hammering on the same question of his grudge against Lynn Trevor, was beginning to infuriate. "You can't prove I've said a word against him—only that once when I turned fool and made a scene at the bank."

"Once was enough," McCoy retorted. "You'd hardly run round publishing the fact, if you meant taking blood-vengeance. Now, getting back to the night of the seventh, you claim to have dined at the Inn with two old friends. That can easily be verified—if true. Where did you go after that?"

"To my sister's," Bob answered sullenly. "Stayed there all evening, reading part of the time. She was sitting up late to finish a dress and I didn't leave till nearly one."

"Who else was there?"

"No one."

"Where was Mr. North?"

"Away over the week-end, on a fishing trip in the Adirondacks."

"You two were absolutely alone the entire evening?"

"Yes."

"M-m. So you've only your sister's word to prove you were there? Might be considered questionable testimony, hers; she's an interested witness."

"I hope you're not insinuating that my wife would lie in a matter of such gravity," Jasper North cut in with a certain chill rebuke. "If she says her brother spent that evening with her, then he undoubtedly did so."

"We haven't heard her say it yet," McCoy snapped back at him. "Though I intend giving myself that pleasure the instant I've finished with this young man," then, with a return to direct questioning: "Say you left the North house a little before one, that leaves the rest of the night unaccounted for. How'd you spend it?"

"Went up to my shack in the woods and to bed, what else would I be likely to do?"

"Anybody with you? Any witness to prove you went directly to your cabin and stayed there?"

"No. I was alone. And this country isn't so populous that I dare to hope anyone saw me going home."

"Humph! So from one o'clock on, the account of your whereabouts depends on your unsupported word?"

"I suppose so—though I will say, Mr. Inspector, that not being an entire fool I'd have had sense enough to plan some land of an alibi, supposing I was really bent on committing a murder."

"Undoubtedly, providing you planned the deed in advance. But it's not so easy to acquire an alibi, once murder is an accomplished fact—say the result of sudden impulse."

"Something could surely be managed with a month to think it out," Bob insisted. "The fact that I haven't the ghost of an alibi for the latter part of the night shows I didn't know the need for one was almost certain to arise."

"M—um—" The Inspector's shrewd blue eyes studied him with a keener interest; he had advanced almost the same thought as that suggested by Tam. "We'll let that slide for the moment and verify your alibi up to one o'clock. Is your wife at home, Mr. North?"

"I believe so."

"Then we'll let Mr. Payne attend to his own affairs for the present—only, young man, I advise you not to try leaving town! Such an act will be considered equivalent to a confession on your part. Come on, sheriff, I'm sure Mr. North won't object to taking us over to interview his wife."

The four men bade their host goodbye and trooped out, leaving him alone with his closely attentive nurse. Even her scanty knowledge of therapeutics warned Tam that the strain of the long questioning had been almost too much for the old gentleman.

"Please let the police handle the case, Mr. Trevor," she begged as he accepted and slowly sipped an offered glass of sherry. "Don't insist on attending any more sessions."

"It's easier to watch the investigation at close quarters than just to sit in the background and think," he told her sadly. "Remember my boy was all I had— His loss—well, I don't think I'm a particularly vindictive man, but I'd gladly give half the remainder of my life to see his murderer punished!"

"Only—that couldn't give him back to us, father dear." Ivy had entered, unnoticed by either of them, and now advanced to lay a caressing arm across the old man's shoulders. "Does it distress you to talk about—about what's going on?"

"Why should it? Either talking, or merely thinking, there's room for nothing else in my mind."

"Then please tell me if they think Bob Payne is guilty."

"That's hard to say. Inspector McCoy hasn't given me his confidence. But surely Lynn had no other enemy, and the Inspector seems to place a great deal of weight on the threats Bob is known to have uttered two years ago."

"Has he any defense, any alibi?"

"He claims to have spent the whole evening alone with Patience; not leaving her, in fact, until almost one o'clock. After that he saw and spoke to no one. The story that he went home and to bed rests solely on his word."

"But surely it doesn't matter what he did after one!" Ivy spoke with a certain urgency, "I was back asleep only a trifle after that time—or perhaps I should say back in bed, for I don't really know exactly how soon I went to sleep."

"*Back* in bed?" her father-in-law repeated, evidently puzzled. "I'm afraid I don't quite understand. You never mentioned having waked up at all during that night."

"Oh, indeed I must have! You've simply forgotten. I'm sure, when we missed Lynn I told you how I'd wakened in the middle of the night and, getting up for a drink of water, had seen the drawer pulled out and Lynn's private papers spilling over its edge! Of course I supposed he'd done it himself, after he came home from the bank, and as his bed was in the further corner, out of sight from where I stood, I naturally imagined he was in it—fast asleep."

"Why, that practically sets the hour, before which the bag must have been packed and the papers disturbed!" Mr. Trevor excitedly pointed out. "It all but proves Lynn must have been dead before one o'clock! How very odd that I don't remember you having told me before!"

"Not so very," she gave him a tender, reassuring little smile. "Just at first, even you weren't worried over his absence and we neither of us realized the importance of small things which happened that night."

"You are sure of the time?" As usual, Mr. Trevor's passion for accuracy poked up an insistent head.

"Quite positive. I looked at the radium-dialed clock on the mantel; its hands pointed at twelve minutes to one."

"It appears to me that, if no one had hitherto told the Inspector of your wakefulness at the precise hour, he should at once be informed. The fact may alter his conclusions."

"So very sorry I neglected speaking of it, to him!" Ivy reproached herself. "I quite thought you'd do so."

"For once my memory failed me, my dear." He stroked the delicate white fingers, on one of which the great opal blazed like a fiery, baleful eye. "If you don't object to keeping an old man company for a little, I shall ask Nurse O'Brien to find the Inspector and repeat what you've just told us."

Tam willingly undertook the suggested mission, and going out to the veranda—where convalescent Paddy wagged a welcoming tail—she looked out across the front lawn and highway toward the North house. While not quite opposite, it was close enough for her to see McCoy's empty car parked at the door; evidently the men were still inside.

She strolled out to the highway and along its tree-bordered edge, meaning to intercept McCoy when he emerged from the house, but before he appeared a tall, bare-headed figure came swinging toward her, so absorbed by his own thoughts that he all but barged into Tam without seeing her.

"Heavens! Doctor, if you must charge along like that, you might at least look where you're going!"

The black head was flung up with something that sounded very like a bitten-back oath, then his responsive laugh effaced her half-formed impression of some barely controlled emotion quite other than mirth.

"Stupid of me, Nurse; you spoke just in time to avoid a collision. Were you looking for me?"

"Only exercising," Tam prevaricated without a qualm, adding: "Do you make it a habit to race along the highway like that? I ask because I'd fancied you rather an indolent sort of person, and your walking most drastically contradicts the idea."

"All depends on the moment and the mood," he parried lightly. "Though, of course, my speed's invariably quite frantic when I'm advancing to an encounter with some lady fair! You see I sensed your approach even though I didn't see you."

"Compliments neither asked for nor required," Tam informed him. "And, chaffing aside, I believe you were deep in some problem just now."

"To be honest, I was," his voice dropped to a serious note. "The whole day's been rather awful, you know, and the autopsy proved something in the way of a last straw."

"Why?"

"Well, it's not exactly pleasant to perform one on your best friend, even assisted as I was, by a competent police surgeon! Also the result leaves us more fogged than before." He hesitated, flinging her an appraising side glance, then evidently decided on frankness. "Not speaking for the police, I personally hadn't much doubt Lynn's murder would prove an open and shut case against young Payne—but dissection of the body says otherwise. Bob Payne's left-handed, markedly so in fact, and has been all his life, yet whoever killed Lynn Trevor struck a strong, right-hand blow; the angle and direction of the wound leave no room for doubt in my mind, or in the mind of the police surgeon who assisted me."

"Rather lets Mr. Payne out, doesn't it? And he's the solitary suspect I've heard anyone mention." She appeared to consider the case aloud, quite as any, untrained but interested young woman might do. "People tell me Lynn Trevor had no other enemy in the world, everybody liked him, and he was positively mad about his lovely young wife; never even glanced sideway at any other women. Perhaps it will turn out not to have been what you might call a 'personal murder,' but just some tramp killing him for his money."

"And then carefully entombing the body—valuables all left in the pockets? To say nothing of a tramp being able to pack and make off with that deceptive bag! Remarkable logic, Nurse, really remarkable!"

"Oh, well, each to his own profession—I never pretended to be a criminologist." Her tone betrayed a touch of offense and, true to his affection for smooth surfaces, Rodney at once set about removing the sting from his last remark.

"After all, your reasoning is plausible, Miss O'Brien. If Lynn really had no enemies other than Bob Payne, and no sweethearts, it does leave a frightful dearth of motive— quite suggests a murder for gain, except that the details don't fit."

"We'd probably better let the detectives work out a solution." She smiled at him, seeming entirely mollified! "But here I've kept you talking for perfect ages, and you were in such a hurry—too bad of me!"

"It was haste with no particular objective, other than a vague intention of looking in to see how Mr. Trevor and Ivy have borne the day."

"Very well, all things considered. She's been lying down most of the afternoon, but I think something to quiet her nerves, so she can get a good night's sleep, wouldn't be a bad idea."

"I'll go in and see them both before dinner."

He left her, disappearing up the Trevor's front walk, and Tam scurried off in the opposite direction; she had already seen McCoy and the Sheriff on the Norths' doorstep and was anxious not to miss the former. As a matter of fact she need not have hurried; they lingered, talking to Jasper North and his wife, whose brother was no longer in evidence.

Tam watched them from a vantage, point on the further side of the highway where she was screened by intervening foliage. What a harsh, sour-natured type Jasper North looked, she reflected, taking out and examining her impressions formed that afternoon. No wonder his wife appeared such a downtrodden, dowdy sort of creature; life with him must be anything but inspiring. She vaguely wondered if "Patience" was her real name, or one bestowed by the country folk as symbolic of her meek, long-suffering wifehood.

Thank goodness, they were leaving at last! Tam signaled the car as it passed her, then told McCoy that she wanted a talk.

"Meet me in the cemetery near the top of the cliff," she suggested. "I'll walk on there at once."

"Good. I'll park by the church. It'll do Dan good to walk home; he's much too plump for proper health."

She had selected that particular meeting place because of its inaccessibility to eavesdroppers. Not that she suspected anyone of undue interest in her movements, it was simply that a detective learns never to take unnecessary chances of having a conversation overheard, and the clifftop, open, and clear of encroaching trees, ensured privacy against unseen approach.

On her way she passed the spot where she had found the opal whose discovery had so far been mentioned to no one, and, noticing that the path forked only a little further on, wondered where the left branch led; deciding to explore it at the first convenient opportunity.

McCoy was already waiting; his dour expression proclaiming anything but a satisfied mood.

"From the look of you, I imagine Mrs. North must have corroborated her brother's story," Tam remarked, sinking comfortably down on the grass, where she sat, cross-legged, looking up at him with what he considered quite uncalled for cheerfulness.

"Even worse—she not only backed up his alibi herself, but the maid-servant, a reliable, God-fearing old woman whom nobody in their senses could suspect of lying, swears Bob spent the entire evening in Mrs. North's sitting-room."

"Poor dear!" She grinned at him with an annoying lack of sympathy. "So you can't clap young Payne into jail, and you've no other suspect waiting to be pounced on."

"Oh, well, there's a bare chance that both women are lying, also their story doesn't cover the night from one o'clock on— There's still enough evidence to justify watching him."

"Sorry to dash your last hope, but Rodney Poole tells me the autopsy shows the fatal blow a right-handed one, and your suspect is markedly left-handed."

"Jumping Saint Peter! Wouldn't you know a nice simple-looking case would snarl up like that!" McCoy complained to the scenery in general. "Here we are, minus a single clue strong enough to bear its own weight!"

"Oh, not quite that bad—there are still a few items worth considering," she encouraged; then, with a sudden gravity: "Mac, you've closely questioned both Mr. Trevor and Ivy about the night of Lynn's disappearance, haven't you?"

"Naturally. Didn't suppose I'd only taken their stories as you passed them on, did you?"

"Of course not. What I really want to know is precisely what and how much concerning that night Ivy told you. Please think back, and give me the gist of her version."

Thus adjured, McCoy abandoned his irritated prowling and sat down beside her, drawing out and lighting one of his atrociously smelling but much beloved cigars.

"Mu-m— Her story starts with a quarrel on that last afternoon, pretty serious one by what she says, though she explicitly refuses to say what it was about. Then dinner, Lynn with the devil's own grouch, and afterwards his departure for the bank saying he'd be detained over some work until late. She waited up, reading, till nearly twelve, then gave it up and went to bed. Only realized next morning when the bag was gone and his private papers mussed about, that he must have come home, packed, and cleared out with devil a good-bye."

"She said nothing of having waked up at some time during the night?"

"Not a word. She distinctly gave me to understand that she'd slept through till morning without a break."

"Same impression I had—until today," Tam nodded. "Didn't it strike you as odd that she was able to sleep calmly through the inevitable noise made by a man hunting around for things and then packing them?"

"Not especially, though I know you spoke of it before. Remember she wasn't in the bedroom itself, but out on the sleeping porch."

"Still, a really devoted wife who'd just had a violent quarrel with her husband would be likely to feel troubled enough to sleep a trifle lightly and wake at the first unusual sound," Tam maintained. "The fact that Ivy did nothing of the kind has always bothered me and today—I'd better tell you precisely what was said. After you'd gone, she came in to ask what we, or rather you and the sheriff, thought about Bob Payne's possible guilt. Mr. Trevor told

her Payne had an alibi up to one o'clock, but nothing covering the rest of the night, and Ivy spoke impatiently, saying
it surely didn't matter where he was after one, her exact
words being: 'I was back asleep only a trifle after that time.'

"Afterwards she altered them to 'back in bed,' but it's
the phrasing of her first sentence which interests me. 'I
was back asleep—' I'm certain I didn't imagine an infini-
tesimal pause between the words 'back' and 'asleep.' Suppose what she really started to say was: 'I was back home
only a trifle after that time?' And suppose she caught herself just in time to change 'home' into 'asleep' without a
noticeable break in the sentence?"

"You're suggesting she wasn't home that night?" McCoy
stared at her blankly.

"Yes! In other words that she was off somewhere on
business of her own which won't bear publishing—and
that's the reason she either knew nothing until morning of
Lynn's departure, or else thought it wiser not to raise an
alarm in the wee small hours."

"Humph! Not much to build on, that. Anybody might
leave the breath of a pause between two words without
really changing a sentence during construction."

"That's not quite all," Tam informed him a bit tartly.
"Though while we're on the subject, I'll add that her silence both to you and to Mr. Trevor concerning this break
in her night's sleep, is decidedly suspicious—and he obviously had heard nothing about it until today when, as I
believe, she made up a story of having waked in the night
and gotten up for a drink of water, simply to cover her
slip about going 'back' anywhere, either to sleep or to bed.
Personally I think she meant back home. Anyway, there's
another item. Mr. Trevor, with his usual craving for exactness, asked if she was certain of the time. And she told him
she'd looked at the radium clock on the mantel—going on
to explain that while she'd seen the disturbed papers half

falling from Lynn's drawer, his bed was beyond her line of vision, so she didn't realize it was still empty and supposed he'd come home and gone to sleep."

"Nothing suspicious about that," McCoy countered. "Seeing the open drawer, she'd naturally take it for granted her husband had turned in without disturbing her."

"Stupid! You've been in their room—don't you realize she couldn't possibly see that clock without also getting a clear view of his bed? Admitted, the open drawer could be seen from the sleeping porch, but not the mantel; to see that she'd have to go well into the bedroom."

"Maybe it was too dark to notice the bed was empty."

"It wasn't—there was a full moon that night, as any detective worth his salt would have found out on first taking up the case."

"That's right—start in teaching me my trade when I've caught more criminals than you've so much as heard about!" McCoy snorted with withering contempt. "What do you think you're driving at, anyway? Trying to dig up clues against Mrs. Trevor?"

"Only hinting at possible undercurrents, old dear, trying to show you the fair Ivy may know a few things she's not telling!"

"Such as what?"

"That's up to you, with your wonderful intelligence and experience, to find out!" Tam grinned at him with the impish mockery that invariably justified her childhood's nickname for him of "Peter-Pepper," and he thereupon promptly exploded.

"See here, Tam O'Brien, I'll thank you not to pull this mysterious, secret-inquiry stuff on me! Either we work together or we don't—but whichever it is, you'll kindly come out in the open and quit dropping hints about undercurrents and held-back information in the part of a woman who's eating her heart out over the loss of her mate!"

"Oh, sits the little bird thusly?" Tam's left eyebrow climbed into a satiric arch. "Has the lovely Ivy really made a conquest of our Mac?"

"Hang it all, Tam, you're enough to make a saint lose his temper," McCoy growled, already half ashamed of his own wrath. "Why the deuce can't you say what you think?"

"Not possible, old dear, since I don't yet know myself." She laughed with unabated good humor. "I only harbor a doubt as to the lady in the case being precisely what she seems and am anxious to verify or disprove my—let's call them suspicions."

"You don't think she has any actually guilty knowledge?"

"Not certain—in other words, I'm sitting on the fence waiting for some definite incident to help me decide which way to jump."

"But, Tam, you can't deny she's horribly cut up. Why, when I questioned her about her husband's last day and evening, she lost her grip and cried like a baby."

"Oh, I'll admit she weeps most convincingly—only— Well, I might as well tell you an incident that I'd meant keeping to myself. You remember, Dr. Poole and I went to break the news while you stayed guarding the body and the sheriff went for a stretcher? Mr. Trevor took the news of his son's murder with marvelous pluck, but Ivy went to bits and had hysterics. I hadn't an idea that her grief was anything but genuine until, happening to glance into a mirror, I saw the reflection of Rodney Poole's expression.

"He was standing behind me so that I couldn't see his face and I suppose he'd forgotten about the mirror. If ever a man's look told of skepticism, half amused, half disgusted, his did then—he might as well have shouted, 'Go to it, Ivy, you're playing the bereaved wife to perfection, but, Lord! if only these others knew what I know!' Now, don't tell me it was a trick of the light or a flaw in the glass,

Mac, for I saw his expression as plainly as I see yours—which, by the way, looks like an incipient thunderstorm."

He ignored the last as beneath notice, only asking: "Any more cards up your sleeve?"

"Not unless you call a lost opal one." She proceeded to tell him of the ring incident, adding:

"You might look into that end, if you will. Just find out when, or if, Mrs. Trevor had the opal in her ring replaced."

She gave him the jeweler's name, remembered from the registered package. "And, Mac, I'd like you to closely question the police surgeon who assisted Dr. Poole. I got the idea Rodney was keeping back something shown by the autopsy."

The Inspector departed, scratching his head.

6
Tangled Ivy

"Do you know whom this belongs to, Agnes?"

The opal found in the cemetery path sat in Tam's extended palm, the morning sun striking iridescent flames from its fiery heart.

"Sakes alive, Miss!" Agnes regarded it, goggle-eyed. "If it ain't the jewel Mrs. Trevor lost out of her ring!"

"Surely you must be mistaken. I've heard nothing about a lost stone."

"Oh, it was long before you come," Agnes unsuspectingly explained. "She lost it the same night Mr. Trevor went away—meaning the night we thought as he went, him really getting kilt, the poor dear gentleman!"

"I suppose she dropped it somewhere about the house, that is if you're sure it was that particular night."

"Oh, I've good cause to remember, Miss. She had us hunting indoors and out, though I made bold to tell her there was no good looking in the grounds, seeing she hadn't so much as stepped off the porch the whole evening and was sure she had it come dinnertime."

"Surely she may have at least gone for a stroll," Tam tentatively suggested.

"For myself, I can't say, Miss, being as it was my night off, but afterwards she said not."

"Then I don't see how this stone can possibly be hers. I didn't find it in the house."

79

She indifferently restored the opal to a place in her uniform pocket, gave Agnes some directions about procuring a particular breakfast cereal for Mr. Trevor's special use, then strolled out the side door and across the grounds toward the cemetery.

So Ivy really had lost the opal from her ring on the very night her husband disappeared! She had worn it at dinnertime and next morning openly announced its loss, telling the maids to search both house and grounds, though only a little later she denied having been outside the house at all during the entire evening. Had she at first seen no reason to conceal the loss of her opal, only later on to realize that to mention it entailed a risk of some undetermined nature?

She had certainly been decidedly vexed, when her father-in-law had commented on the lapse of time since he had last seen her wearing that particular ring; unequivocally declaring she had worn it quite as usual. At this point Tam reached the section of the cemetery path where the opal's response to the sun had caught her attention on that first day in Cedarcliff. It was only reasonable to suppose that, since the opal was found at that exact spot on the path, Ivy had passed along it on the night in question, either on the way to, or from, some destination which she felt necessary should remain a secret.

Which fork of the path had she been following, or about to follow? One fork, Tam knew, led to the cliff-top and from thence by a somewhat devious way to the village. The other? Well, now was as good a time as any to find out where it led.

Cutting away from the side, running parallel to the highway, it meandered between dignified tombs and grassy plots in a generally northwestern direction. It crossed the ravine which later on rose to the cedar-backed cliff, by means of a rustic bridge. Presently, after a good deal of rather aimless wandering, it emerged into what was evidently someone's side garden.

Tam unhesitatingly committed trespass and on nearer approach recognized the Poole house, which she, had already seen at a distance but had not hitherto visited.

It was a pretty, though unpretentious cottage, nestled snugly behind the old cemetery and facing the lane running at the side of the Trevor grounds. Owned by people who evidently cared for flowers, its beds and borders blazed with luxuriant colors, while at one side were massed brilliant clumps of roses, those in the foreground boasting shades running from shell pink to a red so dark as to be almost purple, while those closer to the house and directly under some of its open windows were a lovely, sunny yellow.

Yellow roses!

Into Tam's mind sprang the memory of two such flowers, found crushed, but very little faded, in Ivy's wastebasket.

"Stunning day, isn't it, Nurse?"

The sweet lazy voice cut so unexpectedly across the summer silence that Tam all but jumped. Then, recovering, she turned to see Daphne Poole lying prone on the grass, head pillowed on indolently clasped white arms.

"I suppose I'm trespassing," Tam remarked without much contrition. "Your flowers are so lovely I never thought to look if I was disturbing their owners."

"I noticed you had eyes only for them." She made no move to rise, but lay supinely relaxed, basking in the hot flower-scented air with a suggestion of almost feline enjoyment. "Won't you sit down and admire them at your leisure? I may look hopelessly lazy, but I always retain energy enough for conversation—providing it's not too strenuous."

Never having excursioned into the mind of this particular factor in the case, Tam promptly accepted the invitation, sinking down and offering her cigarette case to Daphne before herself lighting one.

"Thanks, but I'm too comfortable to welcome even so small an effort as smoking." Daphne studied the older girl out of large, shallow eyes, almost as golden-yellow as her hair. "Do you know, nurse, with very little effort you could be almost beautiful—why doesn't your appearance interest you?"

"Why so sure it doesn't?"

"If it did, you'd wear the faintest touch of make-up—a lot wouldn't suit your type—and let your hair grow longer. It's having it clipped so short and smooth that gives you the look of a handsome, frightfully intelligent boy—really your face is ever so feminine and the bone structure's lovely; you'd be quite a beauty if you only put your mind to it! Men don't like our faces to suggest so much cleverness."

"Heavens, child! Is your lecture on my looks meant as instruction in the gentle art of man-catching?" Tam grinned with a really boyish look of derision. "I've heaps better uses for my time!"

"That sounds like Ivy—she's continually railing against the masculine sex."

"Bather surprising in a woman as lovely as she is! I should think all men must admire her."

"Oh, they do, though I'll admit the fact seems to only bore her."

"Well, being so happily married—" the remark trailed off, carrying, the barest hint of a question.

"I wonder?" There was no doubt at all as to the question in Daphne's voice. "How is she taking Lynn's death? You know, I haven't seen her since his body was found. Of course I went over the instant I heard, but Mr. Trevor said she was too ill to see anyone."

"She's better this morning, but still terribly shaken; the blow came as such a shock."

"I know. She was certain he'd only gone off because of their quarrel." With startling suddenness Daphne abandoned her lazy pose, sitting up to clasp her knees, tightly, with an effect of barely restrained energy. "I'd give anything to know what that quarrel was about!" she announced so earnestly that Tam stared. "Any form of row is so unlike Ivy—her way is an accurately dropped, icy bit of sarcasm, then silence!"

"And her husband—was he quick-tempered?"

"Quite the contrary. That's, why I'm so sure whatever caused the trouble must have been something really serious! And you know how it is in a small place—we were all together so much that one hates thinking there were secrets about which one never guessed."

"Everyone tells me they were a supremely devoted couple."

"Everyone would!" Daphne's assenting nod was so vigorous that her golden fluff of a mane fell down into those strange, light eyes of hers and she tossed it back with a murmured word of impatience. "Only—it doesn't seem reasonable for a woman who's really happily married to be so bitter against men as a sex; she never loses a chance of pointing out their pet foibles."

"Yet surely she loved her husband?"

"Oh, not a doubt of that!" the girl's musical laugh held a faintly acid note. "A woman who's not in love seldom indulges in frantic jealousy."

"Frantic?" Tam echoed. "'It's difficult to connect that word with what I've seen of Mrs. Trevor."

"A bit too strong, perhaps, or rather too unrestrained. Ivy's jealousy is of the smouldering, banked-fire type—much more dangerous in the long run. Why—" She broke off to laugh again, this time with what seemed genuine amusement and nothing else: "She was even jealous of me!"

"Why speak as if that was an absurd idea? Most women would be, I imagine!"

"How unkind, Nurse! You must think me a bit of a vampire. Do I really look like a poacher on other women's preserves?"

"Not necessarily," Tam retorted. "You'd only have to run the other way and few men could resist giving chase."

"Meow!" Daphne giggled delightedly. "I see we've another man-hater in our midst."

"Not a bit—I like men ever so much, in their proper place."

"Which, I judge, is never a sentimental attitude."

"That, again, is quite all right in *its* place," Tam conceded. "Only there are so many more interesting things in the world—this problem, for instance, as to why, and by whom, Mr. Trevor was killed."

"Why, isn't it practically certain that Bob Payne did it?"

"There seems to be some doubt. I can't help overhearing some of the police inspector's remarks and he seems far from satisfied. Indeed, I rather hoped your suspicion of another woman might be the real answer."

"Good Heavens! I never breathed a word of any other woman!" Daphne sounded acutely horrified. "I only told you Ivy was frantically jealous."

"She'd hardly be that without some cause, I suppose."

"Why not? Lots of women are. Truly you altogether misunderstood what I meant! As far as I know, Lynn was completely wrapped up in his wife; he never showed the faintest interest in anyone else."

"Being such a close friend of them both, I suppose you'd be likely to know," Tam reluctantly admitted.

"Of course I should—and even if I didn't, Rod would; you know how a doctor automatically gathers all the gossip. You may safely take it as certain that no second woman enters into this case."

Nevertheless, Tam felt far from sure of that fact as she took her departure a few minutes later. There had been the

stress of too pronounced an urgency in Daphne's denial
of any love affair; it hinted at possession of some sort of
knowledge, or suspicion, concerning Lynn's doings, which
she was determined to suppress. Nor did the news later
imparted by McCoy, serve to remove that impression.

He had spent the morning going over Lynn's private
papers, assisted by Jasper North, who, as their lawyer and
one of the two executors of the dead man's will, was chosen by Mr. Trevor legally to represent both himself and his
dead son.

Only letters of a purely social or personal nature had
ever been kept in the drawer in Lynn's bedroom; all the
rest were at the bank and the accumulation, even aided by
the bank employee who had acted as his secretary, consumed several hours of systematic work.

"And it was work we might have spared ourselves. There
was nothing helpful in the lot," McCoy ended his account
of the examination.

"No feminine letters, written by the same hand as the
note we found on the body?" Tam asked.

"Plenty of letters from women, but most of them business and none in the handwriting we're looking for."

"Then, why the-cat-that-ate-the-canary expression?"
she suspiciously demanded. "If his papers gave no clue,
you found one somewhere else."

"Lucky the average criminal can't read my face as easy
as you can!" he remarked with a dissatisfied air. "I was
meaning to hold out on you for a bit, but since you've
guessed that much I'll hand over the rest. In a locked
drawer in Lynn's private safe we found reservation for a
double cabin and two passages on a fast steamer sailing the
ninth of last month!"

"Phew!" Her lips shaped to a silent whistle. "The other
woman!"

"Looks like it, unless Mrs. Trevor can explain! There's been nothing said of an intended journey, but it's possible they planned a holiday trip that fell through because of their quarrel."

"Mr. Trevor would have known and would have been sure to mention it," Tam argued. "I think you'll find there was an elopement in the wind. Has anyone spoken to you of Ivy's intense jealousy?"

"Not the ghost of a hint!" McCoy eyed her with incredulous amazement. "Everybody's sung the same tune—model marriage, model love."

"Yet, as Daphne Poole pointed out today, it's odd for a quite happily married woman to harbor a distinct grudge against the whole masculine sex—and you must have noticed how Ivy always gives them a dig whenever possible." She went on to repeat the gist of her conversation with Daphne. "The girl's a wee bit of a cat, I imagine, but she's no fool, and while she denied the idea that Lynn had been straying into forbidden pastures, I got the impression that was what she really believed—possibly with more reason than she was telling."

"But—" the Inspector's voice was troubled. "Have you followed that thought far enough to see where it leads?"

"Yes—and with the ship passages and double cabin added— It's not so good."

He rose and fell to restless prowling about the study, the room which had been given over to his especial use during the inquiry.

"Given a loving but, as Daphne claims, very jealous wife—a planned elopement which might easily have leaded out, on the part of her husband and some other woman—and said wife's secret absence from home on the night he was murdered. Begins to wear a very murky look!"

"Yet she couldn't have done it alone," Tam pointed out. "Have you talked to the police surgeon? Can he say if there was much strength behind the blow?"

"Not a great deal necessary—the knife used was a fairly short, wide-bladed weapon, heavy and very sharp. He suggests a hunting or possibly a butcher's knife, one of the kind often used in a kitchen. Not much strength would be needed to drive it home."

"Don't forget the subsequent disposal of the body—that couldn't have been managed by a woman, not single-handed at least."

She stopped and they eyed each other, minds obviously questing for a possible accomplice. McCoy, as the more impetuous of the two, spoke first, rather pursuing his train of thought aloud than actually voicing a suspicion.

"Just supposing Daphne feared someone else might tell you that Ivy was jealous of her, so was clever enough to mention it herself, reasoning that you'd imagine said jealousy must be groundless else she'd not speak of it so lightly and out of a clear sky at that. Any notion that she or her brother suspect you're a detective?"

"About Daphne I've no idea. I scarcely know her. But the doctor once or twice has stressed the word 'Nurse' in a way that's made me wonder if he suspects. I never counted on daily contact with a physician when I undertook the role."

"Daphne might steer you off the truth anyhow, just on general principle." McCoy was evidently becoming more and more convinced that Daphne was the missing woman in the case. "Say there was a love affair between the two, and Ivy suspected it—saw those tickets, or learned in some other way that they meant clearing out together—is she the sort to kill him, do you think?"

"I don't know." Tam hated giving a direct opinion unless almost certain of her facts. "Of course she lied about that opal, likewise about seeing the clock on the mantel—and it's practically certain she was out of the house that night. But—mightn't she have simply been spying on her husband and ashamed to confess the fact?"

"Possibly—yet where else do we get a motive for this murder? Bob Payne's cleared, or next door to it, not so much by his alibi as by being left-handed while the fatal blow was dealt by some right-handed person. Then, take another angle, if Daphne's the woman who wrote that love-note we've an accomplice ready to hand. Once Ivy's killed her husband, Dr. Poole would help conceal the body for the sake of keeping his sister's name out of the mess."

"Sometimes Poole does seem to be laboring under a strain," Tam thoughtfully admitted. "And take that look of his I caught in the mirror; knowing that the woman so desperately weeping was really responsible for Lynn's death would explain it. But Mac, we've got to be much surer of our facts before making the slightest move. Such a solution would break Mr. Trevor's heart."

"Can't consider hearts in a murder case," McCoy retorted. "Unless they've been causing trouble by way of a love affair, or somebody's stuck a knife into them! We'll have to get a sample of Daphne's handwriting the first thing; we've got to know if she made that ten o'clock appointment with Lynn."

"Could the night watchman tell you what time Lynn left the bank?"

"No. He saw the lights in the private office burning all evening, but found it deserted when he went his rounds at midnight."

"Did you ask if Ivy'd been to the bank that day?"

"No!" He sounded surprised by the question. "What bearing on the case has that?"

"Possibly none, but if she happened to drop in there and by accident saw those reservations for passages, we'd have a reason for their quarrel that afternoon!"

"That's an idea. I'll ask if she was in the bank on the seventh."

"Are the tickets being tested for fingerprints?"

"No. Bit of an oversight on my part; I failed to realize that just who handled them might turn out important. I'll have them sent to the fingerprint department this afternoon. And Tam, you were right as to something fishy about the autopsy—the police surgeon tells me he's all but certain Dr. Poole concealed some very small object found in, or near the wound."

"Lord, Mac! If he did, that's the most suspicious fact we've unearthed yet!"

"To be honest, I doubted the story," McCoy acknowledged. "Couldn't imagine a motive strong enough to swerve Poole from a straight course—but if his sister's mixed up in the murder, practically the cause of it, in fact—he's plenty of reason for steering the police off the scent."

"It's too early to give your suspicions away by questioning him. Besides, they're too vague to justify any decided move, and there are some contradictory facts that need thinking about."

"Such as?" McCoy cocked an inquiring eye.

"Paddy, for instance. Someone who was very much on the watch, and suspicious of any stranger—even of a trained nurse—must have poisoned him. But Dr. Poole undoubtedly saved his life—he knew exactly what to do and did it instantly, when only a little delay or bungling would have insured the dog's death."

"He'd hardly dare bungle with a trained nurse in attendance," McCoy pointed out. "That was your first meeting and even if he later on saw through your role, he couldn't have suspected you in those first few minutes. It mightn't have been he who knew the dog was a menace, either—maybe Ivy was responsible. Tell you what, Tam, the Poole house must be searched for any traces of tar. Whoever managed the entombment may have tracked a bit of the stuff home on their shoes; though if Ivy did that little thing it won't help much, any tar round the house having already been hooked up with the dog."

"I doubt finding any, after all this time. Oh, did I tell you what the forestry men at work in the cemetery say?"

"No, and I haven't had time to question them."

"They tell me the tree inside which we found Lynn's body was one they had finished treating late in the afternoon of the seventh. In fact, they filled its trunk the last thing before knocking off work. They left both the tar and the kettle and stove used for heating it, close beside the tree. The murderer, or murderers, must have seen the paraphernalia there—perhaps early in the evening, since the people in the neighborhood use the cemetery paths as short cuts—and when the question of hiding the body came up, remembered the tar and the stove ready to hand."

"Rather an inspired idea, I call it!" McCoy's tone held admiration, of a sort. "Only an ingenious brain would think of digging out the tar, inserting the body and refilling the cavity neatly enough so nobody's noticed the tree'd been tampered with. Come to think of it, it's another item pointing to Bob Payne's innocence—he'd never think up such a scheme; simply chuck it in some hole, more likely."

"Of course the tree episode gives us a certain gauge as to the murderer's intelligence, but don't forget rather stupid people develop astonishing cunning when their own safety's at stake. Well, at least the inquiry is opening up— we've more lines to follow than at first! Better not forget to have those tickets searched for fingerprints."

"I'll have the department's report in the morning," McCoy promised. "And in the meantime ask Mrs. Trevor if any trip abroad was planned. Know where she is?"

"When I came in, she was on the side veranda, reading."

"If she's still there, I'll ask her now. Why don't you listen from inside the dining-room window?"

But Tam preferred hearing Ivy's answer from McCoy; eavesdropping was a sometimes necessary evil of their profession for which she harbored scant relish.

Looking a very artist's ideal of the beautiful, disconsolate widow, Ivy vouchsafed the inspector only the barest glance of welcome, quite neglecting to offer him a seat; an oversight which he carefully ignored, taking the nearest chair and regarding her with a look of respectful, intensely sympathetic admiration.

"It seems an imposition to trouble you at a time like this, Mrs. Trevor, but there are some questions only you can answer," he began. "One is, whether or not your husband had made any definite plans about his vacation."

"You mean, did he intend taking a trip somewhere?"

"Exactly."

"He meant staying here at home, with possibly a week-end fishing trip into the Adirondacks. Why do you ask?"

"Because cabin reservations and tickets for England have turned up in his private safe."

"How extraordinary!" Not by the flicker of a lash did she betray any previous knowledge of the reservations in question. "But he must have obtained them for someone else, some client. I'm sure he had no idea of taking any voyage."

"Yet they were good for two days after his death—it's strange nobody claimed them at the time, or has mentioned them since."

"Very strange," Ivy placidly agreed. "Yet I can think of no more reasonable explanation of their being among his papers. Possibly he neglected telling whoever commissioned him to buy them, that they were there." This last she added with the slightly inspired air of a woman who feels she has solved another's problem and at the same time displayed quite unusual intelligence herself.

"Mu-m— That's possible." He was willing, apparently, to accept any explanation of hers; all he wanted was her unqualified denial of any planned voyage.

After one or two more questions he left her and started for the village, bent on settling whether or not Ivy had visited the Trevor bank on the seventh. Only a few inquiries served to show that she had not only been at the bank on that particular morning, but had spent some time alone in her husband's private office; several of the bank employees easily recalled the fact when questioned, as their president's rather mysterious disappearance had served to impress even small events of his last day, among them, rather indelibly on their minds.

So, providing the tickets were not then locked away in the safe, Ivy might easily have seen them, McCoy reasoned. A crime that at first looked like the satisfying of an old grudge, began more definitely to wear the semblance of murder from jealousy, instead.

7

The Face at the Window

Next morning, when the fingerprint department at head-quarters sent word that, while the envelope containing them had been too much handled to render the obtaining of any clear prints possible, the tickets themselves bore the finger marks of at least three men and one woman, McCoy handed over the task of identification to Tam.

"You can get the prints of both women, Ivy and Daphne, without letting them realize what you're after, more easily than I can," he declared. "They're the only two we've any cause to hook up with the case so far—if the tickets weren't touched by either, we're worse off than over. But let's hope for the best. By the bye, my man reports Ivy took her ring into town herself on the tenth of last month—the jeweler has her call, and an order to replace the opal she'd lost, all straight on his books. The job took a bit of doing, as the stone was extra big and she insisted on a perfect duplicate of the original—which she'd bought from the same man; I imagine that's why the ring wasn't back sooner. Begins to look pretty disastrous for the lady, aye?"

"Y-e-s-s—" Tam trailed out the word of assent as though it possessed at least three syllables. "But, Mac, I've grown a whole crop of doubts overnight."

"You would!" Unmixed disgust was in McCoy's voice. "Getting soft hearted because of her good looks, I suppose?"

"Don't be an idiot! It's only that I can't believe she, or any other woman providing she really loved a man, could kill him, hide his body, forge or help to forge the false clue of the packed traveling bag, and then carry on as serenely as she's been doing all these weeks."

"Any alternative suspect to offer?"

"Nary a one," she ruefully admitted, "and furthermore I'm forced to acknowledge that both her actions and a few of Doctor Poole's need explaining."

"Anything particular against Dr. Poole?"

"Just that look I caught in the mirror—one a man who took Ivy's grief at its face value could never wear—and the fact that he suppressed something at the autopsy."

"Pretty slim. I thought you liked the man."

"So I do, with reservations. That in no way prevents doubting his entire honesty. Besides, most men, and quite decent ones at that, would be apt to go a trifle crooked in order to hide their sister's liaison with a married man, not to mention her being the indirect cause of a murder."

"Sure, they would; and what's even more to the point, we've not the ghost of another trail to follow. Nobody benefits by his death—or do they?" he broke off, struck by a new thought. "Heard anything about Lynn's will?"

"Jasper Worth has it," Tam informed him. "He's to read it tomorrow before the inquest. Why?"

"Only wondered if he left much, and to whom."

"His wife, I suppose, though I don't imagine he'd a great deal to leave. I understand his father's the moneyed member of the family."

"Still, if what there is, goes to Ivy, it won't hurt our case."

"It's not a case yet," Tam discouragingly reminded him. "We need a lot more convincing evidence—Ivy's finger marks on those tickets, for instance."

A complete set of Ivy's fingerprints were easily enough gotten from different articles in her room, but the obtaining of Daphne's prints required more care. After duly considering the question, Tam very thoroughly polished a silver compact case of her own, dropped it into the pocket of her nurse's uniform, and then set out for the Pooles' house.

She found the object of her design entertaining two friends, Linda Clyde and Patience North, and looking very much bored by the process. All three women quite openly hailed Tam's advent as a boon, not because of herself, but because of the news she might be expected to impart, and both Daphne and Linda promptly opened fire with a barrage of questions. Most of her answers proved sadly disappointing. No, there had been no new discoveries—yes, Bob Payne's alibi remained unshaken—no, there was no shortage, no money complication of any sort at the bank.

"There you are, actually living in the Trevor house, yet Linda had more news to give us than you!" Daphne reproached her, with the tiniest flicker of malice in her lovely voice.

"Perhaps Nurse hasn't the advantage of being dear Mr. Trevor's closest friend and confidante." Linda bridled with self-congratulation. "He's such a delightful man, and talking over the details of Lynn's awful death with a truly sympathetic listener helps him so much; sensitive as I am, I wouldn't refuse to listen for the world."

"I'll bet you wouldn't," Daphne unkindly agreed. "You'd be more likely to nag for more; anything to keep the 'delightful man' closely attached!"

Tam intervened in the interest of peace and producing the newly polished compact handed it to Daphne, asking if it was hers.

"No, it's not mine." She started to give it back, but Linda, curiosity inspired, clutched it with eager fingers, turning it this way and that until Tam, sure that her unwanted finger prints would obliterate those made by Daphne, felt strongly inclined to slap her.

"Now, whose can it be?" she inquired, finally relin-
quishing it into Tam's outstretched hand. "It's a really nice
case and I don't remember having seen anybody carrying
it. No use asking if it's yours, Patience—you're above the
use of such vanities."

The last was accompanied by a faintly derisive giggle
that brought a touch of angry color into Mrs. North's dull
cheeks, and she flashed a resentful glance at Linda out of
eyes which, Tam noted, were surprisingly violet-blue in
unexpected contrast to her black hair and sallow dark skin.

"My husband doesn't approve of make-up."

It was the first time Tam had ever happened to hear her
speak and the voice, a husky, soft-noted contralto, surprised her almost as much as the amethyst-blue eyes. The
voice suggested a depth of feeling, or temperament, much
at variance with her drab exterior.

"And, of course, the perfect wife never does anything
her husband disapproves," Daphne laughed mockingly.

"Not when the husband happens to be like Jasper,"
Patience retorted. "Or if she does, the mistake isn't often
repeated."

Daphne laughed again, this time with a certain sympathy of understanding. "Yes, there's quite a difference
in husbands—Jasper's always been considered a bit of a
tyrant. But take one like Lynn; nobody could ever accuse
him of dictating to Ivy!"

"She's not at all the type of wife, I, for one, admire,"
Linda re-entered the conversation; a thing she invariably
refused to stay out of. "As I've told Mr. Trevor more than
once, she took her marital duties much too lightly. Ivy
never—"

"LOOK!"

A low, horror-laden cry from Patience cut the ripple of
Linda's speech. "Look!" Her stiffened arm pointed to the
open, sun-filled window—which, as the others turned to

face it, was empty of anything more terrifying than a spray of yellow roses, nodding gently against the screen.

"What the dickens ails you, Patience—seeing things?" Daphne resented the very real thrill of fear caused by the older woman's cry.

"A face!— I saw a face in the window!" Patience stammered through trembling lips.

"Rot! There's no one there!"

Daphne and Tam had reached the window simultaneously and the latter pushed up the screen so they could both look out.

"Truly there was someone!'" Patience insisted. "I saw the face quite clearly—a stranger, probably a tramp." She was beginning to look ashamed of her own terror.

"You must be wrong! There's been no time for anyone to get out of sight."

But Tam, who had looked down at the grass directly below the window instead of searching the scenery for a fleeing figure was not so sure; she had seen a surprising number of blades slowly straightening themselves, as if only just released from some heavy pressure.

Had they been bent under the feet of someone standing to peer into the Poole living room?

Tam repeatedly asked herself that same question as she walked back through the cemetery. It hardly seemed that anyone would dare, in broad daylight, to peer into the room; yet Patience was the only one facing the window, and she had seemed very sure. Again, what possible interest could the little gathering of women hold for any outsider? They had talked of nothing more serious than the ways of husbands, a topic almost certain to arise wherever more than two of the fair sex meet in social converse. There had been absolutely nothing to interest an observer.

Then the sight of a small approaching figure suggested a possible solution. Dips! Perhaps he had been looking for

A low, horror-stricken cry from Patience: "Look—a face!" Her stiffened arm pointed to the open, sun-filled window

her. But Dips promptly denied having gone near the Poole house.

"Sure, I was waitin' for you—but I ain't got so little sense as I'd go peekin' in windows! Think I lost me brains?"

"Did you want me for anything special?" The boy had been given a sort of roving commission, with instructions to casually mingle with the villagers, keeping eyes very wide open and reporting anything of interest to either Tam or McCoy.

"Yep. You know I been givin' the Trevor gardener a hand now and then. Yesterday we done some cleanin' up rubbish and he dug out a little old wheelbarrow fur me— not the regul'r one what he uses, but a dinky, stained little bus—and some o' them stains look t' me like they was blood."

"You think it may have been used to carry Lynn's body from wherever, he died, to the cemetery?"

"More'n like. Supposin' you git a board out of it doc-tored-up at headquarters."

"Can you remove one without the gardener's seeing?"

"Yep. I stuck it way back in a corner—won't be used agin right soon."

"Better give it to McCoy and let him have the stains analyzed," Tam advised. "Anything else?"

"Nope."

She told him of the face Patience North believed she had seen in the window, with directions to watch for any stranger in, or near, the village. Then, as they were about to separate. Dips remembered a neglected item. He dug into his pocket for a tiny, leatherbound notebook such as some men, particularly doctors, carry as vest-pocket re-minders of appointments or prescriptions.

"B'longs ter Doc Poole," he explained. "He dropped it arter he'd carved the corpse." Which was Dips' informal method of describing an autopsy.

"How do you know?"

"Seen him. Soon as he quit powwowin' 'ith you, out in the highway, he ducked into Trevor's and just afore he went up the steps he took out his hanky to wipe his snout. This here book come out, too, and plopped on the ground, so I grabbed it, soon's he went inside. When I seen it was on'y a dinky bit of a book I planned handin' it back, on'y he got in sech a stew over losin' it I thought mebbe I'd better give you a squint at it first."

"What do you mean 'got into a stew'? And, by the way, whereabouts were you that you saw all this? I didn't observe you ornamenting the scenery."

"Sure not! Heaps o' times. I got me eye on you 'ithout you knowin'; just you start a flirt some time and see how quick I turn up!"

"Think I need a chaperon?"

"Not 'ith the men, but you ain't got a heap o' sense about crooks—got no notion as they might pull an iron on you."

Tam had been slowly turning the leaves of the diminutive notebook. It was half filled with medical notations, phone numbers and other apparently unimportant data.

"Take a good look at this?" she inquired.

"Nope, been too blame busy—it was on'y seein' him prance outa the house and do a gallop, nose down, back the way he come, as made me think he hated losin' it. Then yesterday I seen him doin' another hunt, pokin' the grass ter the side of the path and next to crawlin' on the dirt where you and him stood talkin'."

"I don't see why he minded losing it—" Tam began, then stopped as, reaching the back part of the little book, she found two pages stuck firmly together, as if with a drop of glue.

A little careful manipulation and she had pried the edges apart; between the pages was a single short red hair.

It had been partially cleaned, but tiny clotted particles that looked suspiciously like blood still clung, and it was surely the same sticky substance which had held the page-edges together, preventing the hair's falling out either when the book was dropped or during its sojourn in Dips' pocket.

"And he was on his way home from the autopsy when I met him," she reflected aloud. "Looks as if this red hair was the thing he kept from his assistant. What, exactly, did the police surgeon tell McCoy?"

"Seein' it's the first I heard o' it, there ain't no sense askin' me," Dips pointed out with the slightly superior air of one who tries to palliate another's illogic.

"Wasn't asking you, stupid, only thinking aloud. Unless I'm mistaken he said Doctor Poole removed and secreted some small object found in, or near, the wound in Lynn Trevor's breast. A red hair—what was it doing in that position, I wonder? Could it have simply been on his coat and driven in by the knife? Anyway, its presence called attention to the woman he meant to protect; no wonder he impulsively suppressed it."

"Havin' it turn up like this looks a heap worse 'n ef he'd let it be," Dips remarked. "Looks like he'd a good reason for thinkin' it meant more 'n just a shed hair."

"Of course it does, and his being the coroner mixes things frightfully. It seems unfair to spring this on him at the inquest, yet I imagine that's what Mac will decide on doing."

She left Dips and hunted up the inspector, handing him the finger-prints of the two women to be sent in to headquarters for expert comparison, and at the same time showing him the red hair.

"Going to be a queer inquest," he predicted, "with the coroner running a chance of being held for complicity, and his own sister's love affair with the murdered man nearly certain to come out!"

"We've not enough evidence to drag Daphne in," Tam protested. "So far we've no sample of her writing—I tried to get one; wanted her to write down a cake recipe we spoke of, but she was either too lazy or too cautious, said she'd type it and send it over."

"Trust Friend Gossip to help us. Once the possibility of an affair comes into the open, some kind neighbor's bound to volunteer information. Take Linda Clyde for one; if there's been anything of the sort we think going on, she's sure to know."

"But will she, or anyone else, tell?"

"Long odds they will. The average human loves the limelight, even if it's won by branding themselves as the neighborhood's Paul Pry."

"You don't plan asking an adjournment, then?"

"No. I'm in hopes of fresh evidence turning up to strengthen our case against Mrs. Trevor. At present we've too little to make any sort of move. By the bye, your patient's been hunting for you—left word he'd walk up to the top of the cliff and wait there hoping you'd join him."

"Anything wrong?"

"Not that he mentioned; just said he wanted to see you."

It seemed to Tam that the whole day was to be spent in interviewing, or being interviewed by, various people; she badly needed free time in which to think the case over and straighten her ideas before tomorrow's inquest. Still, if Mr. Trevor wanted her help or advice—

She found him disconsolately perched on a rock overlooking the sheer drop of the cliff to the stony brook-bed twenty feet below.

"Are you feeling badly, Mr. Trevor?" Recent habit gave her voice something of the professional solicitous tone of the really trained nurse, and the old gentleman seemed to resent it; he needed advice at the moment, not coddling,

"We can put aside the invalid role when alone, Miss O'Brien. I wanted a business talk with you."

"Of course I'm quite at your service."

"The friend who pointed out your home to me—or to be strictly accurate, I believe he said it belonged to your father, your own establishment being in the city—told me you had the name of never failing on a case. Is that true?"

"Hardly. Such a record would call for superhuman intelligence and colossal good luck. Your friend probably didn't mean his remark to be taken literally—as a matter of cold fact, I've been fortunate enough to count more successes than failures."

"I know you're acknowledged one of the best in your profession. So I hope you won't take it amiss, or imagine I intend casting any reflections—on your ability, when I ask if you're making any progress with the case."

"You mean that as a direct question?"

"I do."

"Then I shall have to tell you, as my employer, that while we're not yet in a position to make any definite charge, both Inspector McCoy and I feel hopeful of being on the right trail."

"You possess clues, or facts, unknown to me?"

"Yes."

"Facts which you aren't at liberty to disclose, even to me?"

"Not at the moment, because most of them belong to the police as much as to me."

"I see—I think I understand." The old gentleman retired into a meditative silence, which held elements of troubled anxiety, to judge by his expression. Tam watched him, wondering if he had stumbled on something which made him suspect his daughter-in-law, or if some new development of which she knew nothing had brought that almost hunted look into his clear dark eyes.

"In that case—since you're not free to tell me exactly how, or in what direction the investigation is proceeding, I fear I must make a most unusual request; I must ask you to consider our business arrangement as terminated, and to drop the case!"

For a second she stared rather blankly, being little used to such casual treatment from her clients. But she was far too generous to be touched by personal resentment in the face of his obvious trouble.

"But why, Mr. Trevor? In what way has my work on the case dissatisfied you?"

"Oh, it's not that—" He sounded harassed and altogether miserable. "I simply feel that my interference was a mistake—I should have let events take their natural course."

"And allowed your son to rest, permanently, under the stigma of being considered a deserter?"

"What's that? I don't follow you."

"If you'd permitted things to simply drift on as they were doing before my entry into the case, your son's disappearance would probably never have been explained, or at least not for years, unless the oak tree where he was entombed happened to be cut down or uprooted by a storm. Remember, while his bag lay undiscovered in the pond, you had no real reason to suppose his disappearance anything but voluntary. The world would have come to believe that he simply deserted his wife and business for some selfish reason of his own."

"That's true, of course," he admitted. "It hadn't struck me in that light."

"Something must have happened to greatly alter your feelings—you once told me you'd give half your life to see his murderer punished!" Tam reminded him.

"Did I? Did I indeed? That must have been said in the first heat of my grief. I feel differently now—feel that it would be much better to let the matter drop."

"It's much too late for that to be possible. Of course I'll withdraw, if you wish it—but the police can't be called off."

"No, I suppose not." He pondered a moment, then said: "Perhaps my request for your departure was a foolish one, which it will be better for us both to forget. I'll feel safer with you on the case—working in my interests—than if the police were handling it alone."

They decided to let it rest at that and walked slowly back to the Trevor, house, talking of everyday things, with no further reference to the investigation. But in Tam's mind, beneath the surface flow of talk, ran an undercurrent of insistent question: What had the old man discovered and what did he fear?

8

"Admit that You Killed Trevor!"

"A queer inquest." Tam remembered McCoy's prediction as she watched one witness after another take the stand, watched the various members of the little group most closely associated with the tragedy, and, most intently of all, the young coroner, on whom official duties obviously sat with such a leaden weight.

Rodney Poole's usually smiling, sweet-tempered expression was veiled by a look of strain. He was nervous to the point of clumsiness, his long surgeon's fingers fumbling whatever they touched in a way utterly foreign, to their usual habit.

Mr. Trevor, Dan Ferguson, Bob Payne, the bank watchman, the minister's small son who had found the submerged bag: each witness contributed his fraction of the story and gave place to the next. Inspector Peter McCoy did not himself take the stand, arranging to have other witnesses place before the jury even such evidence as he had personally acquired, while he himself acted as a sort of unofficial adviser to the inexperienced coroner.

A rustle of subdued sympathy, strongly tinged with expectation, ran along the packed benches, as, the preliminary stages over, the widow of the murdered man was called. All in black, her copper-colored hair almost hidden under a closely fitting little hat, Ivy rose from her place between Daphne and Mr. Trevor, hesitated an instant as if loath to face the coming ordeal, then went bravely forward.

It seemed to Tam's watching eyes that Rodney's fingers pressed Ivy's encouragingly as he handed her the well-thumbed Bible and administered the accustomed oath: "The truth—the whole truth—and nothing but the truth"—

She settled herself in the stiff-backed witness chair, gazing almost indifferently out over the upturned faces; for the platform at that end of the town hall was considerably above the floor level, so that neighbors and curious thrill-seekers alike had an uninterrupted view of the beautiful young widow.

Rodney cleared his throat, fumbled with a pencil, dropped it, and finally cast an agonizing glance toward McCoy, who responded with a reproving headshake. With an effort Rodney banished the outward signs of a consuming nervousness, and began questioning the witness. Name, age, date of marriage. While the answers to his first half-dozen questions were known to practically everyone in the hall, they had to be put for form's sake and once over he speedily settled to the night of Lynn Trevor's disappearance.

"Please give an exact account of what happened that night."

"There's really nothing to tell," Ivy half apologized. "Everything was just as usual. My husband seemed rather quiet, I thought him tired—the weather was terribly hot and he'd been working for months without any vacation— it was to start next day and he planned taking a thorough rest. When dinner was over we had coffee on the veranda, just we three, my husband, my father-in-law and myself; there were no guests that night. Then, about eight or a little after, Lynn told us he was going down to the bank and might stay late, arranging to have everything run smoothly during his holiday.

"After he'd left us, father and I sat on talking for a while, until nine, perhaps. Then he went to his own room and I tried to settle in the living-room. I couldn't read—for some reason the house felt too empty—so I carried the book into my bedroom and read there until a few minutes before twelve. Then I went to bed and fell asleep almost at once."

"So, of course, you had no reason, until next morning, to suspect anything amiss?"

"Not the slightest reason. You see, I woke up after only about a half hour's heavy sleep, and felt thirsty; so I got up for a drink of water, and noticing that the drawer in which my husband kept certain private letters was half open, with some papers spilling over the edge, I naturally took it for granted he had come home while I was asleep, searched for some particular letter and afterwards had gone to bed, as the lights were all out. I'd left a night-lamp burning beside his bed, which was in the inner room, mine being out on our sleeping porch, as I liked fresh air much better than he did, and this night-lamp was also out, so, while not actually able to see his bed from where I stood, I felt sure he was in it, sound asleep. Oh—I looked at the mantel clock as I set back the water glass and it was just twelve minutes to one."

"Now, as we're on the question of lights," McCoy remarked conversationally, the very casualness of his tone serving to disguise the irregularity of his taking a personal hand in the questioning of a witness. "Let's get them clearly straightened out. Your father-in-law went to his room about nine; you stayed for a short time in the living-room, then darkened it and turned on the lamps in your own. Am I right?"

"Quite right," Ivy assented with a faintly troubled air.

"Your reading lamp burned till almost twelve, at which time you extinguished it, leaving only a small night-lamp beside Mr. Trevor's bed. Correct?"

"Yes."

"And did you switch on any lights at all when you got that drink of water—at which time the night light was also out?"

"The moon was very bright. I could see sufficiently without any."

"Thanks. I only wanted to be sure I had the turning on and off of the different lights clearly fixed in my mind." McCoy beamed at her benignly, then relapsed into silence, while the coroner took up his interrupted duties.

"Are we to understand that you had no callers at all that evening, and that you did not go out?"

"Not even into the grounds." Ivy turned to answer him with something of relief; as if she were conscious of a more friendly spirit behind his questions than behind McCoy's. "And no one dropped in. I was quite alone after father went to bed."

Here the Inspector leaned across to whisper something into Rodney's ear. The latter scowled but reluctantly assented, and turned back to ask insistently:

"You are quite certain, Mrs. Trevor, that you remained at home all that evening?"

"Of course I'm certain! Do you think I'd be likely to forget?"

"Sorry to seem a nuisance, but the question appears important." Rodney smiled apologetically. "Now I shall have to ask you to step down for a moment, as we intend calling another witness; but please don't leave the courtroom as I'll probably need to recall you."

As she followed his instructions, Rodney glanced at the paper handed him by McCoy, then he looked protestingly

at his self-constituted coadjutor, who stared back uncom-
promisingly.

"The next witness called is—Miss Linda Clyde," Rodney finally announced.

After the fluffy little lady had taken her place, twit-
tering like a plump yellow-headed canary, and the pre-
liminaries were over, Rodney again consulted the paper
supplied by McCoy.

"Miss Clyde, I must trouble you to think back to the
night of Lynn Trevor's disappearance. Were you at home?"

"All evening!" Linda fluttered reminiscently. "My poor
Agamemnon—my oldest parrot, you know, the one with
the splashes of heavenly blue on his darling wings—was so
dreadfully ill that I couldn't have dreamt of leaving him,
not for a second! Someone, not you, doctor, but some
friend or other, had recommended a strong dose of whis-
key for my cold, and I'd tried taking it but the stuff was so
unspeakably nasty I had to add spoons and spoons of sugar
and even then I couldn't swallow much of it—poor dear
Agamemnon helped himself to what was left and it didn't
at all agree with his constitution. I was up all night!"

"Unfortunate for you, of course; possibly fortunate for
the cause of justice; your sleeplessness may have caused
you to observe some unusual happening in, or near, the
Trevor house. You can see it, and its windows quite clearly,
I believe?"

"Why, you know I can, perfectly, that is the back windows and one whole side. Of course the windows toward
the front and those facing on the lane aren't visible from
my house."

Followed a short silence while Rodney studied the paper
before him with an anything but pleasant expression. Finally
he crumpled it viciously, with a defiant side glance at McCoy.

"You saw no one prowling about the house, no figures
silhouetted against the lighted windows?"

"No strangers, you mean?"

"Strangers or otherwise—did you see any one at all?"

"There's no need to use that tone, Rodney Poole! I'll thank you to remember I'm accustomed to politeness, even from a coroner—and as far as seeing anybody in a window's concerned, how could I, when every single one was dark from nine o'clock till almost one!"

The soft dropping of a leaf might have been heard in the packed courtroom—Ivy Trevor had declared, and repeated under questioning, that her reading lamp had been used from nine till nearly twelve, while Linda Clyde now announced that all the windows overlooked by her had been dark from nine o'clock up to one! And nearly every villager present knew Ivy's bedroom was situated in the house corner most directly facing Linda's cottage.

One woman or the other was lying!

With a helplessly resigned little gesture, Rodney's supple hands seemed to give up control, and he half rose; only McCoy's grip on his arm restraining his very evident desire for ignominious flight. For a minute or two they talked in rapid undertones, then McCoy hitched his chair a little closer to the table and took unofficial, but none the less actual, charge of the inquest.

"Miss Clyde, a good deal may depend on the question of time. Are you positive the Trevor house was completely dark after nine o'clock?"

"As far as I could see, it was," Linda insisted. "Of course the front or lane windows may have been lighted—I can't see any of them."

"But you're prepared to swear those windows to the back, and those facing away from the lane, were dark from nine o'clock on?"

"Certainly! I'd swear to it!"

"You say some of the windows were lighted again at one o'clock?"

"Not quite so late," she corrected him. "I was sitting on my porch, so Agamemnon could get plenty of air, and I grew so sleepy I just nodded a few times: then, all at once, I saw the corner lights in the Trevor house flash on, and I was so interested. I quite woke up— It did seem as if something must be wrong, to have several go on like that in the very middle of the night. But you're a little wrong in the time, it must have been about twenty minutes to one, I think, because they burned for ten or possibly fifteen minutes. And just as they'd gone out Agamemnon had another pain, so I brought him inside and then looked at the time; it was six minutes to one."

"Your clock's usually accurate?"

"Always!" With the bridling of most feminine householders when even mild aspersions are cast on their treasured timepieces.

"You saw or heard nothing else in the least suspicious, on the night in question?"

"Not anything."

"That's all then; you may step down."

Linda rather unwillingly obeyed; she had evidently enjoyed filling the stage center and seemed quite oblivious to the harm her testimony had probably done to Ivy Trevor.

"I fear the court must ask Mrs. Trevor to resume the stand," McCoy remarked with a certain steely smoothness. For an instant Rodney plainly contemplated refusal, then appeared to realize that open defiance might only bring swifter disaster on Ivy's head; it would be tacitly to admit her inability to explain the discrepancy between her story of the lights and that told by Linda.

Only a very close observer would have noticed any change in Ivy's bearing as she answered the recall to the witness stand, a slight stiffness, an almost imperceptible loss of spontaneity, hinted at a guarded self-control. But there was no wavering of eyes or voice as she answered McCoy's abrupt question:

"You heard Miss Clyde's testimony regarding the lights in the windows of your home?"

"Certainly."

"How do you account for the fact that, while you claim to have spent the major part of that evening in your own room, reading, Miss Clyde insists your windows were dark from nine till almost one o'clock?"

"I don't account for it. She either lied, or is mistaken in the night her parrot was ill."

"There is no chance of a mistake in your own testimony?"

"Not the slightest!" Her tone held a certain calm finality that seemed designed to warn him nothing was to be gained by further probing along that particular line. He scrutinized her through half-shut, appraising eyes, then switched to another angle.

"You say you were indoors all evening. Was the dog, Paddy, anywhere about the house?"

"Not that I remember."

"It was only the next day you and Mr. Trevor noticed anything queer in his behavior?"

"Father noticed it. I only felt he was grieving for his master."

"You're fond of the dog?"

"Very."

"Then why did you buy some rat-poison containing arsenic, presumably for the purpose of killing him?"

"Your informant seems oddly careless with facts," Ivy spoke with a faint contempt. "It's true I bought some rat-poison in the village a few days after Lynn's disappearance, but it was at the gardener's request. And the poison contained no arsenic, it was a paste mostly made up of phosphorus with, I believe, a dash of strychnine."

"You didn't, later on, ask Dr. Poole for a small quantity of arsenic?"

"I did not."

"And you're quite unaware who administered poison to the dog?"

"Entirely so."

"We'll let that part slide for the moment, Mrs. Trevor. But there are several others requiring explanation." He leaned toward her, blue eyes boring accusingly into hers. "From the very first, you've maintained that you never left the house the night your husband was murdered—yet on that same night an opal was lost from a ring which you are known to have worn at dinner—an opal you next morning set the maids to hunting, but later on denied having lost. The empty setting was taken, by you, to a jeweler to have the stone replaced and the original opal was afterwards found on one of the cemetery paths—a path you might easily have passed over on your way to the tree where Lynn Trevor's body was callously entombed by his murderer, or murderers! Have you any explanation to offer?"

"I believe I'm hardly on trial, Inspector!" Her delicate lips curled ever so slightly. "And I don't choose to explain any innocent discrepancies concerning my opal."

"Frankness, supposing it to be possible, might be wiser."

"Yes?" Her intonation lent the small word a tang of mockery.

"*Much* wiser!" The inspector looked a good deal closer to losing his temper than she did.

"That you must allow me to judge."

"Kindly remember you're speaking under oath."

"An oath administered by the coroner, not by you. I'm quite ready to answer such questions as he decides to ask."

McCoy hesitated. Technically speaking, he possessed no earthly right to be putting any questions at all; if she chose to insist on strict legality, she might easily refuse to give him any information whatever. Yet there were still several points concerning which he believed he could draw her out more effectually than Rodney Poole could, or would. Just at this point one of his men handed over a scribbled note from Tam:

Don't bring in red hair—will explain later.

He frowningly considered it, but knew his young colleague far too well to neglect such explicit advice, so he merely nodded in her general direction and pocketed the note.

"Your attitude, Mrs. Trevor, shows a strange antagonism to those seeking the truth about your husband's death," he reproved her; incidentally calling the jury's attention to a fact he was anxious they should note. "One begins to doubt the entire harmony of your married life—to wonder if the quarrel which you previously stated had occurred on that last afternoon was as unique as you've led us to suppose. Isn't it a fact that you were intensely jealous of your husband?"

"So far as I know I'd no reason for 'intense' jealousy," she answered with real or perfectly assumed indifference.

"Mr. Trevor was never attentive to other women?"

"Not when I was present—of course I can't answer for what went on in my absence."

"You speak as if a certain degree of indiscretion was only to be expected. Why?"

"Simply because he belonged to the masculine sex— they're hardly noted for constancy!"

"And you're prepared to swear that jealousy had no part in the quarrel which, by your earlier account, was serious enough to make you think it had driven Mr. Trevor away from home without leave-taking?"

"I didn't say that," she countered, for the first time seeming uncertain of her ground; rather as if she hurriedly searched back to make sure just what she had admitted during the earlier stages of the investigation. "I only stated my own lack of the green-eyed passion."

"Meaning that your husband's jealousy caused the quarrel?"

Crash! The clumsiness haunting Rodney's fingers all morning had culminated in the upsetting of a heavy inkwell, which his frantic lunge of retrieval only sent hurtling to the floor, spattering those nearest and generally upsetting the morale of the informal court.

When the inky flood had been mopped up and order restored, McCoy turned back to his patiently-waiting witness.

"Did I understand you to say your husband's jealousy was responsible for this much discussed quarrel?"

"I'm not to blame for what you may see fit to understand!" Ivy retorted. "But I certainly said nothing of the kind."

"You practically acknowledged jealousy was at the root of the trouble."

"Did I?" She regarded him speculatively. "Perhaps you might call it that—people use words so differently. Personally, I'd describe the quarrel as caused by my dislike of another woman; one whom he rather fancied."

"Galloping Moses!" McCoy stared at her, momentarily deprived of breath by her sudden volte-face. "So it was you who were jealous?"

"I don't call it that," she tranquilly informed him. "I only objected to his spending so much time with a girl of whom I didn't approve."

"But that statement directly contradicts your previous testimony," he pointed out. "You declared Mr. Trevor was never attentive to any other woman."

"Not at all—I remarked that he wasn't so in my presence. I said nothing about what happened behind my back, but was perfectly known to me."

"Will you give us the name of this woman in whom Mr. Trevor was—interested?"

"Certainly not. Why drag her in?"

"You were aware that he intended eloping with her?"

At the question, Tam could have sworn an expression of the most complete and perfectly genuine astonishment swept over Ivy's face. Then she conquered all sign of emotion, answering very quietly:

"No. I wasn't aware of that fact, if it be a fact."

"You didn't know he'd already bought the tickets for a fast boat sailing for Liverpool on the ninth of last month?"

"I remember your mentioning some tickets found in his safe, but I've no reason to suppose they were meant for his own use."

"And you never saw these tickets, never handled them?"

"Of course not."

"Then how do you explain the fact that your thumbprint is clearly marked on the cabin reservation?"

She made no attempt to answer, simply looked at him, awaiting his next move.

"Do you still deny having seen or touched them?" She merely nodded and he leaned closer; eyes and tone increasingly threatening. "Why not admit that, already half insane with jealousy, the finding of those tickets acted as the last straw—you guessed they spelled elopement and on that last fatal night trailed your husband to his assignation with the woman for whom he meant to jilt you—then—either in her presence or after they'd parted, you accused him of unfaithfulness and, driven mad by his admission, took vengeance into your own hands—" He paused a second, closely watchful of her reaction, then went on, his voice suddenly deepening to a note of sympathy. "Such a story, frankly told, would win the sympathy of every man who heard it. Why not trust yourself to the jury—why not confess the truth?"

"I might, if there was one atom of reality in this fine web you've spun!" Ivy's voice rang chill, faintly contemptuous. "As it is, I refuse to confess a lie!"

"You persist in asserting entire innocence?"

"Most certainly I do, since I'm actually innocent."

"Then why have you lied from the very beginning? Why insist you spent the fatal evening at home, when your lost opal and darkened windows prove the contrary? Your story of having waked in the night, thirsty, is earmarked false by the testimony of the lights which a neighbor swears were fully on at the very time you claim to have seen your husband's disturbed papers solely by the light of the moon! Even your own lips contradict you—the statement that you saw the clock on the mantel clearly enough to read the time while failing to notice that your husband's bed remained empty is manifestly a lie—the room is so arranged that you couldn't see the mantel without at the same time seeing the bed! Why not admit the truth? Your thumbprint on the ticket proves you knew of your husband's planned departure—the evidence of the lights proves your entire version of your actions a tissue of falsehood—even the mute evidence of your wheelbarrow, its boards soaked with human blood, goes to prove you used it to transport your husband's body to the place of his secret entombment!—Mrs. Trevor, take my advice, give up a losing battle—confess—and throw yourself on the mercy of the court!"

White to the lips, but with proud little head still bravely erect, Ivy rose to face him.

"Accuse me as you like, even arrest me—I won't confess to a crime I didn't commit!"

"You assert innocence, in face of the overwhelming evidence against you?"

"I do!"

"Then blame only yourself for what must follow. Step down, please—we'll call other witnesses."

As she turned toward her former place, something in her pale, undaunted beauty so stirred Rodney that he forgot prudence, forgot himself, forgot everything but the superb courage of the woman accused; he sprang to his feet, offering his arm with an almost courtly respect. She accepted it, flashing him a warm smile of thanks, and so escorted crossed the platform to Mr. Trevor's side.

Meanwhile, McCoy had called the name of another witness: Bruno, the Trevors' gardener. A grizzled-haired, rather stupid-looking man shambled slowly down the aisle between the bench rows, and mounting the steps stood hat in hand, gazing first at McCoy then at Dr. Poole, as the latter resumed his official seat behind the coroner's table.

With a disgusted gesture Rodney washed his hands of the whole unorthodox proceeding, and the Inspector found himself compelled to administer the witness' oath. That, and the opening questions regarding name, age and occupation hastily disposed of, McCoy settled to the real business in hand.

"Now, my good man, you identified the small wheelbarrow shown you by Sheriff Ferguson as one recently left standing in the tool-shed at the Trevor place?"

"Yes, sir."

"A board from this wheelbarrow was removed and sent to headquarters for analysis," McCoy here explained to the jury. "The chemist reports the stains disfiguring it to have been made by human blood. Now, Bruno, can you tell me when you last used this wheelbarrow?"

"Yes, sir, t'were the day before yesterday, when me and a boy as does chores round the place used it for lugging rubbish."

"And before that, when was it used?"

"I couldn't say as to that, sir."

"Well, if not the precise date, can't you give us an idea if it was used before or after young Mr. Trevor's disappearance?"

"I couldn't say, sir." He seemed unnecessarily troubled by the question, his brown eyes darting furtively this way and that, finally settling on Ivy with a look of acute distress. Catching that look, McCoy promptly read into it a reluctance to disclose something damaging to his young mistress, and eagerly pressed the point.

"There must be some way of fixing the date, at least approximately—try to remember for what purpose the barrow was last used. That may help."

"But I can't, sir!" Bruno helplessly protested. "I didn't ever see that wheelbarrow until a week or two back, when I found it a-setting in our tool-shed!"

"Found it? What the devil do you mean?"

"Just that, sir—the one belonging on the place is considerably bigger. This here little one were tucked away in our tool-shed first time ever I laid eyes on it."

"Then why did you identify it when shown the barrow by Sheriff Ferguson?"

"He asked did I know it, and I says sure I did, but nothing wasn't said about it belonging to our place—which it don't."

"You don't know who it does belong to?"

"I do not, sir."

"Very well, you may step down."

But this Bruno appeared unwilling to do. He restlessly crossed and uncrossed his feet, emitting weird snorting sounds as he glared frantically from the Trevors to Dr. Poole and back again, finally choking out a few incoherent words which McCoy was unable to understand.

"You'll have to speak up, my good man, I can't hear you."

"Please, sir, could I be give a chanct to tell what come to my knowing, that night as Mr. Trevor got killed?"

9

Why Paddy Barked

The gardener's request sent an excited hum along the crowded benches; was it possible that this hitherto unimportant witness might cast some new, perhaps lurid, light on the tragic mystery of Lynn Trevor's fate?

"You know something about the events of that night? Something you haven't told?" McCoy eagerly demanded.

"There wasn't no call to go talking afore now," Bruno defended his silence. "A loose tongue's got a-many into trouble—'sides, what come my way of knowing ain't so much, 'cepting it kinda shows the mistress weren't the only one a-prowl that night."

The inspector caught at the implied admission. "You know she was out of doors?"

"Not myself, I don't," Bruno unhesitatingly contradicted. "I was just naturally going by all the 'provings' you talked about, and if she were I wanted you to know there was others."

"How do you know that?"

"'Cause that night as Mr. Lynn got himself killed, I was out to the Inn real late—checkers we was playing, and afterwards drank some of what they sells for beer. 'Long about half after twelve I come ambling home real easy like, count of it being so late. Close to the garage where I sleep, I was, when I hears Paddy putting up an awful row. So,

123

thinks I, he's heard me—but 'twasn't that, he was making
for the house, and for a man I was just able to see a ways
from the sleeping porch door.

"Paddy got real close afore the man spoke to him, sharp
but soft-like, and the dog quit his noise and give a little
whimper like he always does to a friend. So, thinks I, it's
Mr. Trevor or Mr. Lynn, out for a breath of air and I went
on inside—not watching any more. But it warn't neither
one of them."

"Why so sure?" McCoy could not resist the temptation
of cutting into the rather long-drawn-out story.

"Next morning I seen the man's tracks," Bruno carefully explained. "We'd a new-planted flowerbed just past the
steps to the sleeping-porch door, and it were all tramped
up—I knowed neither one of my gentlemen would ha'
walked on it like that, and anyhow, whoever squashed
them seedlings carried a bigger foot than what they done."

"Had both Mr. Trevor and his son unusually small feet?"

"They had, sir, the both of them, not so long as most
and a lot thinner."

"And this stranger's feet were noticeably larger?"

"They was, sir, though as to his being a stranger I'd not
be wanting to bank on 't."

"Why?"

"Well, it was this-a-way. Arter Paddy hushed his fuss
and I went on in, I got feeling peckish—that beer we'd
drunk hadn't no manner of body to it, as could fill a man—
so I fixed me a snack in the pantry and after I'd et it, made
for to get to bed. Being as my bed's by a window looking
on the lane, I cast out my eyes at the weather the last
thing—it 'ud be around one, or close to it, by then—'twas
a big-moon night and the lane real lit up, so I couldn't
miss seeing a man mouching along like he'd just left our
side gate. Thinks I, 'tis the same as Paddy barked at, and
with that I dropped to me sleep."

"You recognized this man in the lane?"

"I did, sir."

"Who was it?"

"Do I be duty-bound to tell that?"

"It's your duty as a citizen to answer any and all questions bearing on the murder of young Mr. Trevor!"

"I was only planning to show that there was other folk about— But if I've a

duty to tell more, I'll own I knew the man in the lane by the height of him, the way he walked, and the air of a tune he's the habit of whistling soft-like— It was Mr. Rodney, no other!"

"You're ready to swear to that?"

"I am, sir."

To McCoy, the inference was obvious. From a possible accomplice, Dr. Poole suddenly loomed as an equally possible principal; what had he been doing just outside the sleeping porch door at twelve-thirty—only a few minutes before the time at which Linda Clyde had testified the lights in the Trevor bedroom flashed on? If only Bruno, less easily satisfied by Paddy's friendly greeting, had watched to see whether he had entered the house! Again, the time when Rodney was seen in the lane fitted with suspicious exactness; supposing he had entered Lynn Trevor's room, hastily packed the deceptive traveling bag, for some unknown reason rummaged through the private papers, and finally extinguished the lights at six or seven minutes to one—the time Linda claimed the windows had again gone dark? He could just comfortably have reached the spot in the lane indicated by Bruno, at the time given. And most suspicious fact of all, why had he never mentioned this midnight visit to the Trevor house, if it was of an entirely innocent nature?

Yet this new evidence; McCoy knew, while to a certain extent implicating Rodney Poole, did nothing toward clearing Ivy. If her account of her own actions held any truth at all, she was in the sleeping porch, awake, between twelve-thirty and one o'clock; by no possibility could she have remained ignorant of Rodney's hypothetical visit. Coolly looked at, it seemed that Bruno's testimony instead of casting any beams of helpful light, merely deepened the general murk.

McCoy's brief reverie was abruptly shattered by the emphatic falling of the coroner's gavel.

"This travesty of an inquest has lasted long enough!" Dr. Poole suddenly announced. "The police have been given every possible facility for rounding up their case, supposing them to possess one. As coroner, I intend curtailing further inroads on the time of this judicial body— Gentlemen of the jury, I ask that you render a verdict!"

"Just a moment, Mr. Coroner!" the inspector heatedly began. But Poole cut him short with another thump of his gavel.

"We've wasted enough moments! Mr. Foreman, do you need to retire for consultation?"

After an exchange of serious whispers, the foreman declared that they did not; the jury had already formed a unanimous opinion. Duly rendered, the opinion went down in the inquest records as a verdict of "Wilful murder committed by a person or persons unknown." And with that finding McCoy found himself compelled to rest satisfied—temporarily at least.

Permission for Lynn Trevor's burial being given, his body was that same afternoon consigned to a second, and it was to be hoped more permanent, resting-place.

The funeral once over, McCoy and Tam retired into the privacy of Mr. Trevor's study for serious conference.

The inspector's temper, always a trifle peppery, had been so soured by the premature ending of the inquest, that Tam rather expected a stormy session. Her impish streak, seldom far below the surface, set a mocking light dancing far back in her smoke-blue eyes.

"I tell you, Rodney Poole's a damned dangerous man!" McCoy stalked indignantly about the room, his hair ruffled from angry fingers and his whole expression threatening explosion. "Look how he choked off the inquest, once the facts implicating him began cropping up! Bruno's testimony must have been the devil's own shock—up to then he'd probably no idea he'd been seen."

"You've thought out a motive?" Tam, who watched him from behind a protective screen of cigarette smoke, mildly inquired.

"Doesn't require much thinking!" he loftily assured her. "It's obvious that Poole discovered his sister's love affair, jumped on Trevor about it, they fought and the stronger man killed the weaker—not much gray matter needed to think that out!"

"Sorry to disagree, old dear, but we've been harking down the wrong trail— Daphne and her affairs are really the least of his troubles."

"Now, what in hell do you mean by that?" McCoy came to a pause directly before her, to stand glowering down at the slim, lounging figure, much as if he longed to shake it. "Think he killed Trevor for some other, more personal reason?"

"Much more personal," Tam nodded, "that is if he killed him at all, which I muchly doubt. Judging by present indications, I'd say Lynn unfortunately learned of his wife's love for Rodney, and that caused the quarrel we've heard so much about; but I don't think it had an earthly thing to do with his death."

"Holy Mackerel, Tam! You're crazy!" the Inspector wrathfully exploded. "It was Lynn who'd gone on the loose, not Ivy!"

"Don't be too certain! I believe they were both doing a bit of straying, probably quite unknown to one another. Of course, the scrap of note found in Lynn's pocket pretty well proves he was carrying on some sort of clandestine romance; but on the other hand her secret absence from home rather hints at irregular activities on her part as well. And I'm increasingly sure she and Rodney are in love."

"In the name of Heaven, why? I've never seen a damned thing to suggest it."

"You wouldn't! You're a man and less versed in the small ways of women. For instance, you were present last night when she sewed a button on his coat; I suppose it told you nothing whatever?"

"What the devil could it tell?" McCoy flopped help-lessly into the nearest chair and automatically dug for a cigar; he needed its soothing stimulation.

"Whenever you see a woman's needle busy with some garment belonging to a man, watch her—that is if you're anxious to learn her inner feelings about that particular male," Tam pityingly enlightened him. "I've seen a girl, supposedly madly in love with her husband, stab his sock so viciously while darning it that I wasn't in the least sur-prised to hear they were divorced only a few months later; in fact I wouldn't have been greatly astonished at the news that she'd murdered him. Now, when Ivy sewed on that button, she petted the coat, if you know what I mean; her fingers took caressing curves, even her needle was thrust gently, lovingly, through the cloth—only love makes a woman sew in just that way. If you doubt it, watch the next mother you happen to see mending the clothes of some adored tot."

"Mean to say that's all you're going on when you say they're in love?" he incredulously demanded.

"Not all, but frankly it was the deciding item. You know I've been worried since the very first as to why Ivy didn't hear the person who packed that bag—even supposing she was peacefully asleep, as her first story proclaimed. Then the episode of the lost opal was decidedly suspicious, and since she made that slip about being 'back' by one, changing what I still think started to be 'back home' into 'back asleep,' I've entertained very little doubt that she was really elsewhere at the time in question—some 'elsewhere' which grave reasons made it imperative should remain a secret. Naturally I wanted to find out where she'd been and watched closely for signs of any outside interest.

"The first day here, I found two badly crushed yellow roses in her wastebasket. They weren't faded, simply crushed, and when I got to thinking about them afterwards it seemed to me that flowers worn on a woman's dress when she was embraced with more emphasis than discretion, would be crushed in a very similar way, and—those roses were much too fresh for said embrace to have been administered by her husband, who'd already been absent for three weeks. Rodney, being a very presentable specimen of his sex, and a constant associate, seemed the most likely lover in sight; so I watched them together and soon hadn't much doubt—they're far too careful not to have something to hide."

"Humph! Sounds all right," McCoy grudgingly admitted. "Though it strikes me as fairly slim, and even supposing you're right—the fact of their love only strengthens the plausibility of joint guilt."

"Think so?"

"Yes, I do, and what's more I don't see why you've done such a sudden switch—you were all for Ivy's guilt a little way back!"

"More or less. I was fishing for the most probable suspect—still am, in fact—and if we believed the marital jealousy was all on her side, the indiscretion all on his, then there really was a strong possibility that Ivy had killed him and Dr. Poole had aided her to cover up, because of the wish to protect his sister's good name, supposing her to be the second woman in the triangle. But once amputate Ivy's jealousy and we've got no motive for the crime; a woman's hardly likely to slay an erring husband in a fit of jealous rage, when her own affections are actively engaged elsewhere. Not stating that my present opinion is necessarily final, at the moment I think the lovers were simply together the night of Lynn's murder, and all their suspicious actions since then have been attempts to conceal that fact. Remember, if they really are perfectly innocent of his death, they'd scarcely visualize themselves as likely suspects—their own secret meeting would be the only thing to strike them as needing concealment. And if you'll go over their conduct by the light of that suggestion, you'll admit there's nothing to contradict the theory."

McCoy lapsed into a dour silence, apparently rehearsing the case as Tam had advised, while she watched him with the flicker of an amused smile hovering around her beautifully-cut lips. Suddenly he arrived at some thought which afforded him intense satisfaction, and emerged, chuckling triumphantly.

"You've left out that red hair, Miss Know-It-All! Can't tell me a thoroughly innocent man would suppress material evidence as he suppressed that hair found in the wound! By the bye, why'd you send the note advising me not to bring it out at the inquest?"

"Wanted? to prevent a blunder, old dear. Remember, just before that the evidence had dealt with Paddy and who'd poisoned him? Well, while listening, the reason for an oddity I'd noticed about that red hair came to me— It isn't a woman's hair at all, it's a dog's!"

"The hell you say! But its color's identical with Ivy's! I've not had a chance to actually compare them, but that dull, coppery red's unmistakable."

"It's a color she and Paddy boast in common," Tam assured him. "I noticed how exactly his coat matched her hair the very first time I saw them together—and if you'll closely examine the red hair you're so carefully treasuring, you'll notice that while it's about the correct length, it hasn't one sharply cut end, as a woman's bobbed hair ought to have. I wondered at the fact, but hadn't sense enough to realize the true reason until Paddy was forcibly recalled to my mind."

"Maybe you're right, maybe not:—I'd best get an expert's opinion. Anyhow, whether that hair came from dog or woman, I still think the pair of them guilty—more than ever now we suspect they're lovers! And I'd thank you to tell me what grounds you've got for setting up a different opinion."

"Not a great deal," she admitted, reflectively consulting the tip of a freshly lighted cigarette. "Anything peculiar strike you in Bruno's testimony?"

McCoy mentally skirmished back. But he could think of nothing fitting her description, and frankly acknowledged the fact.

"In telling his story, Bruno mentioned a newly planted flower bed 'just past the steps to the sleeping-porch door.' He told how it had been trampled, presumably by the man at whom Paddy had first barked, then had welcomed as a friend. Bruno failed to question that that man, and the one he afterwards saw much more clearly in the lane, were the same person—but doesn't it seem curious that Rodney shouldn't know the exact location of those steps, especially on a moonlit night? He's in the habit of running in and out of the Trevor house like one of the family. Between the inquest and the funeral I got Bruno to show me just where he'd seen those footprints, and whoever left them—pointing in the direction in which Bruno insists they pointed— would have had to pass the sleeping-porch door and go on toward the corner of the house. But he is sure the prints only went part way, then turned back."

"So you deduce that the trespasser wasn't too sure of his ground—in other words, he hadn't Poole's entire familiarity with the house doors and their precise location?"

"Exactly. By Bruno's own account, he saw the man very indistinctly—must have, because he at first thought it one of the Trevor men and only later decided it must have been Rodney, and there's certainly no similarity in the height or build of those three men. Again, Bruno said nothing at all of the man in the lane carrying a bag, yet you've been taking it for granted it was to obtain that article that Rodney's midnight visit was paid. Scarcely seems reasonable that he'd pack it, hide it somewhere on the premises and return for it later."

"Humph, there's something in that. What's your reconstruction of events?"

"I imagine Lynn was in the habit of using night work at the bank as an excuse when he wanted a long, free evening—a habit Ivy had noticed, and took advantage of to keep secret appointments of her own. She was still absent, somewhere with Rodney, when whoever killed Lynn came, bent on manufacturing misleading evidence of his victim's voluntary departure. How he knew she was absent, I can't say; perhaps he didn't, and simply took a chance of not waking her—anyway I think the murderer was this visitor Bruno saw the first time. While the gardener was satisfying his hunger, this unknown finished packing the bag, for some reason went through Lynn's private papers, and calmly departed, turning out the lights a few minutes before the time given by Linda.

"He must have barely got clear of the house before Ivy returned, escorted by Rodney. They evidently didn't linger over their leave-taking, else Rodney couldn't have been in the lane as quickly as Bruno saw him there. Judging by the latter's description—he says Rodney was strolling along, whistling an air he's fond of—Dr. Poole hadn't an idea anything was wrong. But Ivy must have taken alarm, to some extent at least, when she entered the bedroom and found it tossed about—more than probably she later told the truth when announcing her belief that Lynn had voluntarily disappeared because of their quarrel. Anything in my attempted reconstruction that strikes you as far-fetched?"

"N-o-o—" McCoy blew a cloud of smoke ceilingward. "Only trouble is, it leaves us no nearer a solution than at the start! You've suggested no alternative suspect, or mo-tive."

"For the last, I've nothing to offer; and for the first, only the vaguest kind of a suspicion. Did I tell you how Patience North insisted she saw a strange face looking into the Pooles' window?"

McCoy recalled the incident, but refused to admit it had any bearing on the case.

"One never knows what may turn out vitally import-ant," Tam retorted. "So I've had Dips keep a special watch for strangers, on the chance. Heard anything along that line yourself?"

"Not a whisper."

"Neither have I, except through Dips. That kid has an uncanny power of discovering carefully hidden facts. He tells me a tall, well-dressed stranger, driving an extremely expensive high-powered car, has been haunting the vicinity ever since he's been on the lookout. Of course, this stranger doesn't openly appear in his car, but parks it somewhere out of the way and hangs about the outskirts of the village, particularly the cemetery, for the best part of every, or at least every other night; then toward morning he returns to his car and drives off, apparently, without having seen or spoken to a soul. Dips is all at sea as to what he's after."

"Maybe a reporter, or a private sleuth hunting clues," McCoy offered helpfully.

Dips had seen a mysterious stranger, who drove an
expensive and speedy car, leaving the cemetery in
the small hours of the morning

"In the dark, and without interviewing anyone?"

"Probably hasn't yet connected with the right person."

"That's more like it—I'd give a good deal to know just who's the attraction."

"Doesn't sound a bit promising. You're off on a wild-goose chase, Tam," he admonished. "Better stick to the suspects in hand. Nothing you've brought forward convinces me of their innocence. Frankly, I'm going after their scalps—both red and black. Better trail along."

"Can't, Mac, I feel too doubtful of their guilt, particularly Ivy's."

"Sure you're not prejudiced by her beauty and her winning ways?"

"Not a scrap! But stick to it, old dear; I'll admit you've much more to back your theory than I have against it. All the same, I mean landing Dips' prowling stranger and learning what's attracting him to this neighborhood. I'll let you know if I come across anything definite."

"That's the worst of female brains." McCoy surveyed her pityingly. "Even the best of them hate sticking to a straight line—they're always tempted off at a tangent. Well, here's where I get busy hunting up evidence to confirm or disprove your theory of a secret love affair between Ivy and Dr. Poole! Say, if that turns out to be true and Lynn also was carrying on with Daphne, they did keep it strictly in the family, didn't they?"

He departed, chuckling, and Tam permitted herself to fall into a train of thought so deep that she failed to hear the soft opening of the study door and remained unconscious of Ivy's entrance until she spoke.

"So, I've unconsciously found a champion in the enemy's camp!" Such was Ivy's conversationally voiced remark. Tam frankly jumped, then stared at her suspiciously.

"You were listening!"

"Of course I was," Ivy quite shamelessly confessed. "Wouldn't you, if your honor, perhaps your life, was the stake?"

"Almost certainly," Tam smiled at her. "Though I don't see how you managed it—that door looks decidedly solid and I happen to know it was tight shut."

"Ah, a skillful eavesdropper scorns anything as obvious as a keyhole or door crack. Besides, I discovered years ago that if the hot-air register in this room is opened, any conversation held here travels through the furnace pipe to an attentive ear not too far away from the dining-room register. It's sometimes proved a convenient method of listening in—so knowing the inspector uses this room, I simply opened its register when there was no one watching. Today's not the first time I've overheard a talk between you two; only, hitherto, there's been nothing to make me seek any closer touch."

"And they accuse detectives of using underhand methods!" Tam reproached her.

"It all depends on the motive; I've merely been trying to guard myself and the man whom, as you've already guessed, I love."

"So I wasn't wrong in that deduction?"

"Nor in any other, as far as I could tell. May I ask if you believe in my innocence enough to actively help me?"

"I daren't make rash promises," Tam hedged with a detective's instinctive caution.

"At least you'll let me speak quite frankly?"

"More than that—unless I find some definite reason to believe in your guilt, or in Rodney Poole's, I'll do my utmost to prove your innocence!"

"Thanks!"

Only one word, but it held such a depth of gratitude that Tam more than ever believed her a victim of unfortunate circumstances rather than a criminal—no guilty person would hail such a qualified promise of assistance with fervor, for only conscious innocence could make a suspect sure that nothing more than skilled help was necessary in order to establish that innocence.

Ivy sank into a chair close to Tam's. "You've no idea what a heavenly relief it is to speak out!" she sighed. "Life's been a perfect nightmare ever since Lynn's body was found."

"You guessed suspicion was pointing your way?"

"Of course, and the fact that I'd been with Rodney that night horribly tied my hands; it almost forced me into clinging to the original story I'd told before anything having happened to Lynn occurred to anyone."

"If I'm to help at all, you'll have to be perfectly frank," Tam warned her. "And let me ask all the impertinent questions I see fit."

"That's understood. And besides, you've already discovered the one secret I've been struggling to hide—my love for Rodney." Suddenly she laughed softly, more genuine amusement than bitterness in the sound. "To think how I agonized because my heart had turned traitor to Lynn, when all the time he was pleasantly dallying with some other love!"

"You honestly had no idea he was unfaithful?"

"Not the faintest!" And Ivy's tone was so earnest that Tam found herself believing it. "Cold, grouchy, more or less tired of me, yes, I knew all that—but I hadn't the least idea there was any other woman."

"And no suspicion, now, as to who she may be?"

The soft coppery hair whose color had so nearly deepened Ivy's trouble, was shaken by a puzzled negative.

"I've tried my best, but there seems no one at all. As far as I know Lynn never looked at a woman; my testimony at the inquest was only meant to distract attention from my own sins."

"I guessed that, also that Dr. Poole upset the inkwell as a warning that you were telling too much."

"Perhaps I was a tiny bit rattled," Ivy acknowledged. "The Inspector had rather got me in a corner with his harping on jealousy—my jealousy, he meant, but if Rod hadn't given me a cue that I was wrong, I'd probably have admitted Lynn's jealousy caused our last quarrel. After that, I quite brazenly switched my whole attitude, if you remember."

"Wouldn't it be wise to tell me about that quarrel; and the tickets?"

"How on earth did you guess a connection?" Her gold-flecked brown eyes widened in an amazed stare.

"Just guessed it." Tam grinned at her with encouraging friendliness. "Your fingerprint clearly proved you had handled those steamer tickets. Yet you seemed so unimpressed when the fact came out, I thought you must have handled them under circumstances that could bear explanation. Probably they openly appeared in your quarrel with your husband."

"They caused it, or at least brought it to a head! Lynn had been ragging me for months past about seeing so much of Rodney—while he seemed no longer to love me himself, he strongly objected to my interest in anyone else; quite in the usual masculine way."

"Probably it's their sense of ownership that makes them such dogs in the manger," Tam heartlessly agreed. "Don't you think they're usually much better friends than lovers?"

"I hope, indeed I believe, that Rod gives me a wonderful combination of the best in both relationships." Ivy's beautiful face was so illuminated by the ardor of her faith that Tam promptly acquired the information she was seeking: this woman really loved deeply, idealistically, it was not simply a fleeting passion.

"Let's hope he's the one shining exception. But so far you haven't enlightened me about those tickets."

This was the tale the footprints told—the whispered conference at the edge of the cliff, the struggle, the crashing fall to the creek bed below, the woman who turned and fled light-footed through the night

10

Hurled from the Cliff

"Lynn found the tickets in my desk, which I'd been care-less enough to leave unlocked," stated Ivy. "He accused me of planning to elope with Rod, and while I didn't ex-actly admit it I don't think he entertained much doubt. There was a horrid row, naturally—the poor man's feelings must have been further complicated by the fact of his own secret liaison. Well, in the end he took the steamer tick-ets away with him—the next morning, when I realized his departure, I thought he'd used them for an impromptu trip abroad."

"What prevented your carrying out of the original plan of your own elopement?"

"I hardly know. Partly Lynn's open accusation, I sup-pose, partly the fact that it seemed doubly mean to sneak off during his absence."

"Wasn't it only because you'd been with Dr. Poole that you lied so disgracefully about never having lost the opal?"

"Certainly! I never dreamed Lynn had met foul play and was only amused when father's fussing over his ab-sence culminated in his secretly hiring a detective."

"So my role of trained nurse didn't deceive you?" Tam chuckled softly.

"No. Rod discovered the deception that first night, when you helped him with Paddy. Next day he told me

you were an extremely clever young woman, but not well
enough versed in the medical jargon to be really a nurse.
Since father had tried palming you off in an assumed character, we easily guessed his anxiety about Lynn had ended
in his engaging a private detective to investigate, and
a few quiet inquiries settled the matter—you're a fairly
famous person, you know."

"Mr. Trevor never told me I'd be in daily contact with
a doctor, or I'd never have attempted the role. But after
all your guessing doesn't matter, now. Tell me, have you
thought at all about the dog's poisoning?"

"You mean that, happening on the very day of your
coming, it suggests someone else also knew you as a detective?"

"It may have been a coincidence," Tam's tone was dubious. "But it doesn't seem likely. Heavens! This case is
enough to drive me to drink or drugs! Now that you and
Dr. Poole are practically cleared, as far as I'm concerned
at least, there simply isn't anyone to suspect! Hadn't your
husband any enemies at all?"

"Not that I know of—if you exclude Bob Payne," Ivy
assured her after a moment's thought.

"Oh, he's out of it—left-handed, to say nothing of an
alibi—I wonder—"

She straightened, intently following a new line of
thought. "Would it be possible for a left-handed person
to strike a glancing blow in such a way as to deceive doctors, two of them, into thinking it had been dealt by a
right-handed person?"

"I've no notion. Suppose we ask Rod. But why the question?"

"If such a thing *is* possible, Payne's innocence rests
only on his alibi—I think I'll use some of my spare time
trying to shake that. Is his sister the type of woman who'd
lie to save him?"

"I imagine so; they're ever so devoted—but the old servant is honesty itself." Entire conviction rang in Ivy's voice, "And you remember she backed up Patience's story of having spent the whole evening with her brother."

"I remember." Tam slumped disgustedly back into the depths of her chair. "All the same, I'll ask a few questions at the Worth house if opportunity offers. Bob Payne and the stranger with the high-powered car are literally our only hopes. Never did I see such a dearth of suspects!"

"High-powered car?" her hostess echoed interestedly. "That's someone I hadn't heard mentioned, before I listened to you from below."

Tam repeated her own very limited knowledge, in the hope that Ivy might be able to shed some light on the possible identity of the prowling stranger, but Lynn's widow could think of no one who might, by the wildest stretch of the imagination, be expected to feel enough interest, either innocent or otherwise, to haunt the neighborhood.

"It seems one of those times when we detectives have to either fold our hands and wait for blind chance to turn up a new lead, or else begin again at the very beginning," Tam sighed. "And patience not being one of my shining virtues, about two more days of this disheartening failure will surely send me harking back."

"Perhaps Rod and I can help. I may tell him you've become an ally?"

"Yes, if you're careful not to let anyone else know—not *any* one."

Ivy had barely time to give her promise of discretion before Mr. Trevor called her from the hall. Linda and the Pooles were on the veranda, and she went to join them, so that the two women had no further chance of private talk.

After thinking over the case until her brain felt fuzzy, Tam decided on joining forces with Dips. Perhaps between them they could corner the elusive stranger or at least get

a good look at him. Not long before midnight the boy
brought word that the stranger's car was parked a half-
mile from the main highway, but that he himself was no-
where to be found.

"You at least got his license number?" she asserted rather than asked.

"Not that bird's, I didn't!" was Dips' disgusted retort.
"He's hitched two mismated plates on his car, one twenty-
two and t'other twenty-four—by the look he drug 'em out
'a junk heap—course they'd keep or'nary folk from noticin'
like ef he run a bare car, but they ain't helpin' us any."

"Wonder if it's best to simply wander round on the
chance of seeing him," Tam meditated, "or do you know if
he has any special haunts?"

"Mostly hangs 'round the cemetery and the church.
Trouble is, he sees or hears you comin' quicker 'en a mos-
quito—I moves pretty soft and kin see in the dark to beat
hell, but I ain't got close enough fer a good squint yet."

They decided to cut through the cemetery toward the
church and the rectory, which faced it across the highway,
and, keeping to the darker side paths to avoid being seen,
had gone about halfway when the boy suddenly pulled
Tam behind some bushes, motioning her to silence. She
had heard no unusual sound, but knowing Dips' phenom-
enal powers of hearing, guessed he had detected something
or someone. Even by strained listening she heard nothing
beyond the ordinary night sounds of the country; softly stirring leaves, strumming insects of the darkness, and
sleepily whispering night winds; but presently her eyes
caught a vague moving shape—a woman wrapped in some
dark garment who stole noiselessly across the grass.

It was too dark to see clearly and her head appeared to
be muffled by a veil or scarf, so that it was impossible to
hazard a guess as to her identity, but they slipped quietly
after her, hopes high that at last the elusive owner of the

high-powered car was to meet whoever brought him to
that neighborhood.

Just behind the church was a fairly thick wood, which
their quarry entered, Tam and her small lieutenant following as closely as they dared. Describing a half circle
through the wood, the woman approached the church from
the side nearest the village, where trees and shrubs grew to
within a few feet of its wall. There she paused for several
minutes as if listening, then went closer, finally reaching
a window which lay in such deep shadow that the watchers
could no longer make out her exact movements, but a very
faint creaking sound suggested that the window was being
cautiously opened.

Dips touched Tam's arm, signaling her to stay quiet,
then he dropped flat on the ground and commenced crawl-
ing noiselessly forward. He had gone only a short distance
when sudden pandemonium broke at the church window—
the woman they had followed screamed sharply, then fled
back toward the wood, while at the same instant a man
leaped out through the now wide-open window and dashed
away in the opposite direction. "Follow him!" Tam cried.
"I'll go after the woman."

The wood was so dark that had her quarry observed
anything like the stealth used in her approach, Tam could
never have picked up her trail. But the sound of hastily
brushed shrubbery acted as a guide and she soon caught
sight of the fleeing figure.

Lithely active and always in carefully maintained condition, Tam could safely count on outdistancing most
feminine runners. They had covered only a few hundred
yards before the distance between quarry and pursuer lessened so perceptibly that the former evidently despaired of
escape. She suddenly checked her headlong pace and
leaned, panting, against a tree, waiting for Tam to come
up with her.

Night breeze sleepily whispered
through the tombstones—Tam saw
the moving shape of a shrouded
woman who stole noiselessly across
the grass

"Any especial reason why I should be chased like a runaway child?" she angrily demanded.

"You!" Tam stopped short, for the voice was Daphne Poole's.

"Why, Nurse O'Brien! Nobody told me you were a trained runner!" A carelessly laughing note rang through the words; her first anger was either gone or most beautifully hidden.

"And nobody warned me you had the habit of wandering the countryside at night!" Tam retorted. "I quite thought I was following some mysterious thief, bent on robbing the church altar."

"Oh!" Daphne hesitated, apparently uncertain as to her best line, then she covered the pause with another laugh. "So you were attracted by queer noises in the church—just as I was."

Tam dodged a direct answer. "What were the sounds like?"

"As if somebody was moving about very softly; and I thought I saw the flash of an electric torch."

"How on earth did you happen to be on this side of the cemetery so late?"

"I might easily ask you the same question."

"Oh, I was simply on my way home from the village," Tam lied casually. "When you screamed and a man jumped out of the church window, I certainly thought the place was being robbed. That's why I ran after you."

"What became of the man? Which way did he go?" Daphne questioned, forgetting to hide her almost breathless eagerness.

"I didn't notice. He went so fast I knew it was hopeless to try catching him."

"So you picked me as a victim! Ever so nice of you; I'm sure. You scared me out of at least seven years' growth."

"You thought I was the man, giving chase?"

"Naturally! I'd no reason to suppose the churchyard quite so populous. Was there anyone else around?"

"How should I know? And you haven't yet told me what the man was doing or who he was."

"I haven't the least idea—it was so dark I couldn't see at all distinctly. It was only hearing somebody in the church at that hour that made me try to investigate; and a pretty shock I got for my pains! Next time I can't sleep and cultivate Morpheus by a stroll, I'll take care to stay nearer home."

They had walked along one of the cemetery paths while talking and now reached a fork where their homeward ways parted. The light was slightly stronger, there in the open, and Tam unkindly took advantage of it to survey Daphne's carefully cloaked figure with an openly appraising eye. A spoken remark concerning the oddness of her costume for a summer night's stroll was quite superfluous. The look spoke volumes.

"Good night." Daphne turned away. "I hope the chase didn't tire you."

"Not at all, and I'll reciprocate by hoping you won't suffer again from sleeplessness."

"Thanks, but I'm almost sure to—it's a bad habit of mine—did I hear you mention guilty conscience?" And with another laugh flung back over her shoulder, she disappeared in the direction of home.

Tam went on to their usual meeting place, settling down there to await Dips' return from the chase, and his report. So Daphne Poole was also interested in the elusive stranger! For that it had been he who had leaped from the window, Tam entertained no manner of doubt. What exercised her mind was the question as to whether Daphne had been spying on him or keeping an appointment with him. The balance hung fairly even between the two possibilities—she remembered it was at Daphne's window

Patience North had seen the peering face, and she recalled Dips' report that the cemetery seemed the stranger's favorite stamping ground.

Was he simply trying to communicate with Daphne, and did the whole thing mean no more than another secret romance?

Here Tam sighed impatiently. She was getting extremely tired of all these clandestine loves, known or suspected—

If only people would restrict their affections to tame legal channels, how much trouble the world at large and detectives in particular might escape! She had always suspected something feline underneath Daphne's dainty, dresden-china beauty, and because of it was now more inclined to imagine some sinister reason for her interest in the unknown than she might otherwise have been. Could they, one or both, be in any way connected with Lynn Trevor's murder?

The girl's dark cloak and muffling veil loudly proclaimed that she had expressly dressed for the midnight excursion, and that fact, together with her stealthy method of approaching the church, seemed more indicative of spying than of appointment—unless some very serious reason lay behind the latter; a girl seldom goes to a mere lover's meeting so garbed and with such intense caution. Here Dips' arrival broke up her train of questioning thought.

"Led me all over hell's kitchen and then done a fade-away!" he bitterly complained. "Gee, but that bird can run!"

"He made his car?"

"How should I know? I tell you he lost me! When I'd done ramping round tryin' to pick him up and made for his car, it was gone—he'd parked it somewhere else, or druv clean away."

"No use hunting him any more tonight," Tam decided. "We'd better both turn in."

"You catch the lady-bird?"

"Oh, yes—it was Daphne Poole."

"No!" Dips straightened, his eyes wide with surprise. "Suppose it's her he's been tryin' to connect 'ith?"

"Perhaps, or perhaps she was watching for him just as we were."

"Notice she knew darned well where to look! And say, what was he doin' in the prayer-hall—think there was anybody 'ith him?"

"I don't know," Tam ruefully admitted, "and I can't imagine what made him pop out the window like that—of course he may have heard it being opened, but you'd think in that case he'd naturally run away from it, not toward it. Oh, let's give it up for tonight and go to bed! There'll probably be something else to worry us by tomorrow."

She hardly guessed how true a prophecy the words were to prove. Breakfast was barely over when Dips broke all rules by boldly appearing at the front door and asking for Miss O'Brien.

"Sure, I know I wasn't to let on knowin' you," he apologized at sight of her disapproving frown; "But this here's somethin' extra special—couldn't let the bird cash in whilst I hung round waitin' a chanct to see you private!"

"What in the world are you talking about?" Tam inquired as she followed him down the veranda steps and out on the side lawn, away from possibly listening ears.

"Man in the brook!" Dips cryptically retorted. "Do we let Mac in on this, or do we swing it on our own?"

"If you'd give me an idea what you're raving about, I might be able to say! For Heaven's sake, calm down and explain what's happened."

"Our bird didn't do a getaway last night or else he come back later—I just now found him in the cemetery brook. Must 'a' fell off the cliff—at first off I thought he'd croaked, but he's still breathing, so mebbe we kin bring him round enough to talk."

"Dips, you're a heartless little savage," she reproached him. "Only thinking of making the man talk, instead of what he's suffering! You think he's badly hurt?"

"Pretty well smashed up, but it don't matter so long's he ain't dead. Whatcha waitin' fer?"

"Thinking what's it's best to do." She hesitated, then turned back toward the house. "I'll phone for Dr. Poole and to the inn for Mac. That's the quickest way."

Dips, openly disgusted by such humane regard for the stranger's comfort rather than for what he might be able to tell them, awaited her return. Then the two hurried on and, gaining the cemetery, scrambled down to the bed of the brook, following its western bank until they neared the spot directly under the steep cliff which gave the village its name. There a man lay motionless, his body half submerged in the shallow water, either unconscious or dead.

With a pitying murmur Tam kneeled beside him. First assuring herself that he was still alive—had he been dead she was far too experienced to disturb his position before the coming of the police—she lifted his bleeding head to her knees.

He had almost certainly fallen from the cliff above. One leg was crumpled under him at an unnatural angle that showed the bones must be broken. His head had struck against a stone with such force that Tam feared the blow must yet prove fatal. She gave Dips her handkerchief to wet in the brook and bathed his face, but otherwise made no effort to revive him, guessing that a return to consciousness must mean intense pain.

It seemed an age before Rodney Poole arrived, and another before the coming of McCoy, the sheriff, and two men with a stretcher. It proved impossible to get the latter down to the brook's edge, so they were compelled to carry the wounded man to a more gradual incline and so up to the cemetery level. Dr. Poole's skilled hands steadied the broken leg during the ascent; but even so, the motion caused pain severe enough to penetrate the clouds of merciful oblivion and bring the stranger back to hideous agony. He shuddered, feebly trying to clutch his tortured head as they laid him on the stretcher and forced a needed stimulant between his clenched teeth.

"Hold hard, old chap!" Rodney encouraged, as the slow cortege started away from the brook. "Better take him to my house—it's nearest and I'll have him under my eyes—it's going to take some watching to bring him through."

For a little, the man seemed again to lose knowledge of his own pain. Then, as they neared the cemetery wall, he opened unseeing eyes and began struggling as if determined to rise.

"Only give me strength!" he half sobbed. "I'll wait—I *will* have patience—only give me strength!"

With the last words he lapsed into a merciful stupor, from which he did not rouse during the setting of the broken leg and dressing of the terribly injured skull. Dr. Poole held out scant hope of his recovery.

"He must have landed directly on his head," he declared. "Quiet and careful nursing may bring him around, though I warn you it's doubtful. However, I'll do my best."

Later on, Tam and the Inspector went through the contents of the wounded man's pockets in search of evidence as to his identity and data regarding friends or relations who should be notified of his condition. From letters and personal cards they learned that he was Ronald Dunn, of Milton, Massachusetts, a lawyer.

In view of the fact that both detectives felt fairly certain he was the mysterious stranger who had lately been haunting the vicinity—an opinion later borne out by the finding of his expensive car parked in a little-used lane—

McCoy decided on sending a man to Milton to make inquiries concerning him, in the hope that some link between him and the murdered man might be discovered.

"And if there's a link, it'll turn out to be through Ivy," he predicted. "Lynn's murder may be something that's reached out of their joint past."

"A la Anna Katherine Green," Tam twitted him with an unbearable hint of old-fashioned methods, then, before he had time to explode, hurried on. "It's only fair to warn you that, after last night, we've more reason to suspect Daphne Poole of being in some way connected with the gentleman from Milton. Come outside and I'll tell you what Dips and I stumbled across." She proceeded to give him a detailed account of their midnight excursion and its result, ending: "Of course he simply changed his car from one parking place to another, and came back as soon as we'd left the coast clear. Question is, did Daphne also venture out again?"

"We'll have a look at the cliff-lop and see if it has anything to tell us," the Inspector decided. "Too bad I didn't think of putting a man to watch it, so these everlasting thrill-seekers wouldn't get the chance to tramp out any footprints at the place he fell from."

"Don't worry, I imagine news of the accident hasn't yet reached the village; there's hardly been time."

A moment or two later she was proved wrong, for Patience North met them and at once asked about the injured stranger.

"Poole's patched him up and kept him as a resident patient—says he thinks saving him's a matter of doubt."

"Oh! I was told the fall had killed him outright."

"Close to it, but not quite," McCoy assured her.

"It seems so odd for a stranger to be wandering about the cemetery at night!" Patience commented. "He is a stranger, isn't he?"

"Oh, yes, but doubtless when news of the accident spreads about, somebody'll come forward and claim him."

"Perhaps I'd better go and ask Daphne if there's any way I can help."

She left them, going on toward the Poole home, while Tam and the Inspector continued their interrupted way.

Unfortunately, most of the ground closely adjoining the cliff-top was too grass grown for the retention of any clear footprints. But a few spots of bare earth held more promise; in one of them McCoy discovered a distinctly marked woman's print.

"Humph! Looks as if Miss Daphne came back," he remarked, well pleased by the find. "Anything along where you are?"

For a second Tam failed to answer, then she only called him across to a strip of clay-like soil on the very lip of the cliff.

There was no need for comment; what lay there told its own story.

A man's footprints, and a woman's, passed from the grass to the dirt side by side and stopped as if the two had chosen that spot for a discussion. The woman's prints went deep, showing she had stood for some time without moving—the man's blurred right and left, even registered several mixed impressions as if he had shifted uneasily about—then came two backward feminine steps and a masculine forward stride, the prints moved, sideways, even nearer to the cliff's edge—mingled first one then the other on top, indicating that the two had struggled at close grips; then, abruptly, the woman's prints stood clearly out—alone.

"By the sins of Saint Peter, she pushed him over!" McCoy uttered. "See—here's where she turned and ran, light-footed—only her toes to the ground. Tam, if that man dies, somebody's going to face a charge of murder!"

"Let's hope it won't come to that! Surely Rodney can save him."

"Maybe; I'm not waiting to make sure—a sketch of these footprints and casts of the clearest ones have to be made today. Mind watching them while I go to the Trevor house and phone headquarters?"

"Of course not—I'll wait as long as you like."

He vanished after a hurried "Thanks," and Tam sank, cross-legged, on the grass, fished for a cigarette and lighting it, gave herself to a train of absorbing thought. A close observer, who also knew her well, might have detected the dancing of a tiny green flame far back in her blue-gray eyes—the flame which always, with her, spelled a newly born thought or discovery of some vital clue.

When McCoy came back, she welcomed him with such pleased animation that he eyed her with dawning suspicion.

"What's happened, or what're you up to, Tam O'Brien?"

"Awful to have such a suspicious nature; I'm ashamed of you, Mac! Can't a person enjoy a lovely summer day and the country quiet without being accused of hatching some fell design?"

"Lovely morning be hanged! You're planning some devilment," he retorted unconvinced.

"Honestly, I haven't seen a soul," she told him with perfect truth. "Did you get headquarters?"

"Yes. They're sending out men to photograph and take casts of the footprints. Ferguson will be here in a minute to stand guard until they come."

"How about sending a man to the stranger's home town?"

"I got Laney detailed for the job; he's to report here for details and a look at the injured man before starting."

"Oh, well, Laney's not so bad," Tam conceded. "But his long suit is following a trail once it's pointed out to him, rather than picking up new scent."

"If you think he's so stupid, why don't you go yourself?" he inquired, nettled by her slur at one of his favorite men.

She only smiled with irritating sweetness. "Who knows? Perhaps I shall."

11

Tam Turns Burglar

"He's still alive, that's about all that can be said." Daphne sounded politely depressed by the gravity of the report given in answer to Tam's question. But nothing in her manner suggested the least personal interest in the man hovering at death's door; if he was really better known to her than to the others, she was concealing the fact with consummate skill. It was the second day after the finding of the stranger from Milton, and he still lay unconscious, attended by Dr. Poole and two trained nurses. Tam, who had walked over to inquire as to his condition, accepted Daphne's offer of tea, which she was pouring on the rose-bordered side lawn.

"Does your brother still hope to save him?"

"He's not saying definitely. But Rod's a very good doctor, even if he is my brother; he'll pull him through if it's at all possible. Lemon or cream?" The last as she deftly prepared Tam's cup.

"Lemon, please."

For a little they talked lightly of this and that, neither mentioning anything more serious than the proper brewing of tea or the rival attractions of different sorts of icings, then Tam ventured a reminder of the promised recipe which the other had failed to send.

"I meant typing it, in the interest of clearness, but my machine's been out of order," Daphne apologized, with the sweetest of smiles hiding an undernote of malice.

"Why not use handwriting, then?" her guest casually suggested. "I'm ever so good at deciphering temperamental writing."

"Oh, mine's not that," Daphne laughed softly. "In fact it's so pretty I never waste it on commonplace things like cake recipes—and never by any chance give samples to people whose reason for wanting it I don't quite trust!"

"You speak as if you included me in that horrid category."

"Oh, dear, no!" the girl protested, her lovely yellow eyes wide with shocked surprise. "Only, you see, Rod warned me long ago as to your real profession, so I feared somebody might have absentmindedly signed the wrong cheque or written an indiscreet love note, and you imagined my writing might help you decide who was responsible."

"If you're always so careful, and never spread it about at random, there's surely no reason to be afraid."

"Of course not. All the same, I think that recipe must wait till my machine is mended."

There was no use persisting; Daphne quite evidently did not intend parting with any samples of her writing, so Tam surrendered the point and passed on to another.

"Ever since the injured Ronald Dunn was found, I've been wanting to ask if you saw him again after you and I separated in the cemetery."

"Again?" Daphne echoed. "Why, when had I seen him before?"

"Surely it was he who jumped out the church window."

"Heavens, do you think so?" blank amazement sounded in Daphne's tone. "You'll probably think me frightfully stupid, but such an idea never occurred to me."

"No, I don't believe I'd call you exactly stupid." Tam's words and smile cheerfully admitted defeat. "Though perhaps I do think you'd be more clever if you were more frank."

"I always think it's ever so satisfactory to talk with somebody who can entertain quite different opinions from one's own and yet bear no grudge. I'm beginning to feel that you and I shall end by becoming fast friends—Nurse."

Surely trying to question the fair Daphne was sheer waste of time. Tam gave it up and presently returned to the Trevor house, where she found McCoy indulging in a fit of the blues.

"There's no head nor tail to this damned case!" he bitterly complained, glaring at Tam quite as if the fact were entirely her fault. "Every clue that turns up wanders round in circles, then either dead-ends or peters out to nothing at all."

"What particular clue has been misbehaving itself now?" she sympathetically inquired.

"Don't you call it maddening to have an injured man stick unconscious when his talking might clear up the case?"

"Optimist! How do you know he has anything valuable to tell, or that he's even connected with our murder?"

"Stands to reason he wouldn't have been hanging about otherwise—to say nothing of getting pushed off the cliff. But that's not all, everything else's on a par! Why, I can't even start a house to house hunt for the shoes that made those prints; got to have some solid grounds before I show any woman she's suspected of attempted murder by demanding to see all her footgear—and while I'm hunting an excuse the guilty party's had plenty of time to destroy them!"

"I thought you were too certain of Ivy's and Rodney's guilt to bother over other suspects."

"So I am certain, or anyhow next door to it—all the same, there're side lines in the case that need looking into. Take that blood-stained wheelbarrow as one; appears nobody ever saw it till it turned up in the Trevor tool-shed—you'd think it walked there of its own accord!"

"Did you ask if any of the village stores had sold it?"

"None of 'em ever saw it!" he responded dismally. "Or if they did, they don't remember; yet Lord knows it must have come from somewhere."

"Why don't you arrest your chosen suspects and trust to clearing up the side issues afterwards?"

He cast her a withering look. "Because I haven't enough evidence for a jury, and well you know it! No use arresting unless conviction's pretty sure to follow."

He went on disconsolately grumbling, but Tam gathered that he really intended making no decided move until Laney's return from Milton, and with the idea of distracting his mind, suggested re-examination of the anonymous wheel barrow. They had already gone over it, but not with quite the minute thoroughness they now employed; it was Tam whose inquisitive fingers discovered, and finally dislodged, a tiny flat oval of tarnished silver firmly caught in a crack between side and bottom of the dilapidated barrow.

"What is it?" She displayed the tiny bit of metal on her extended palm.

"Looks familiar," McCoy regarded it with a thoughtful eye. "Where am I used to seeing little oval plates like that? a jack-knife," he presently announced, pleased at having captured the elusive memory. "Most decent grade pocket-knives have a plate set in for initials."

"Too bad the owner of the knife neglected inscribing his," Tam regretted. "It won't be much use in tracing the murderer, but it may come in handy once we've landed our criminal; it's the sort of thing a jury likes. May I keep it?"

"Certainly. When I can't find the owner of a thing the size of this confounded barrow, it's not likely I'd be any luckier with a morsel like that. Keep it by all means."

For several days nothing of importance developed. Ronald Dunn continued to hang between life and death, his lips locked by unconsciousness. Tam did a little unobtrusive investigation on her own account, though, like the Inspector she was awaiting Laney's report before starting serious action. McCoy and the sheriff chased elusive clues which brought them no nearer their goal.

On the fifth day Laney returned from Milton with a most uninspiring report. No one with whom he had talked had ever even heard of either the Trevor or Poole family, and the reputation they gave Ronald Dunn was almost insipidly virtuous.

Wealthy, successful, ambitious, he had never been known to glance at a woman with eyes of interest, much less indulge in a love affair; he never gambled, fought or drank—in fact he was a most model young person, whose fair name had never been touched by the faintest breath of scandal.

"Humph, sounds too good to be true," was McCoy's comment when he had listened to a detailed account of Ronald Dunn's virtues. "It's not natural for any decent looking youth to be quite that bread and milk—suggests he's got some hidden vice up his sleeve."

"But I tell you he's lived in this town of Milton all his life." Laney felt called upon to defend the accuracy of his own report. "If there were any dark secrets in his life somebody'd surely know."

"Not a doubt of that, Laney; only question is, did you happen to miss the right 'somebody'?"

"That's a question I intend trying to answer," Tam informed them, "I think I'll take this afternoon's train for Boston. Milton's close outside that city, isn't it?"

"Practically part of Boston; the two run more or less into each other, with Dorchester sandwiched in between," Laney answered. "Milton's an independent town—one of the richest in America, I was told. But what's the idea, Miss O'Brien? Think I've fallen down on the job?"

"Not precisely—I just happen to know, or perhaps I should say, suspect, a few facts about Ronald Dunn that weren't included in the data supplied you by Inspector McCoy. My inquiry will probably follow a slightly different line than yours, that's all."

When Mr. Trevor heard that Tam was leaving them, he anxiously insisted on her definite promise of return.

"Not being altogether blind, I couldn't avoid seeing which way the wind blew at the inquest," he sadly informed her, "and since then I've gained the impression that you're really Ivy's friend. I'm afraid of what may happen if Inspector McCoy is left here alone."

Instead of reassuring him Tam asked a question: "I wonder if you'd mind telling me exactly why, on the eve of the inquest, you suggested my withdrawing from the case."

"Sorry, Miss O'Brien, my motive was one which I feel hardly at liberty to divulge. At some future time, perhaps—" The sentence trailed into embarrassed silence.

"I asked more for your peace of mind than my own," was her enigmatic response, and there the subject dropped.

During the four or five days of Tam's absence nothing in particular happened. McCoy spent hours on the trail of the ownerless wheelbarrow without gaining a particle of information concerning it, and other equally fruitless hours in search of the murder-knife, which had so far remained in successful seclusion.

On the Saturday a wire from Tam announced her return that evening, but it failed to mention that her train reached New York well before dinnertime, or that she was meeting her father for that meal and a strictly private consultation.

Over their coffee she requested the big Ex-Chief of Detectives to desert his beloved Westchester farm long enough for a visit to the Adirondack mountains.

"You know you'll enjoy the fishing and a little detective work will do you good."

"Precious little you care about the fishing! All you want is some information that you think I can collect easier than you could."

"Don't pretend you're not enchanted by the thought of getting back into harness," she retorted. "It's just like a man to try and acquire credit for doing something he thoroughly enjoys."

"Where you ever got such contrary ideas about my sex beats me!" Rance O'Brien sighed resignedly. "You'd think, being brought up mostly by men, you'd have more respect for us."

"That's precisely the reason I see through your little ways," she retorted with an affectionate side glance. "Never mind, dad-dear; a nice conventional daughter who did what she was told and considered all men as superior beings wouldn't amuse you in the least. Think how much more fun you get out of me and my cases."

The remark held enough truth to silence him. The conversation ended, as Tam had known it would, in his consenting to take the desired trip to the mountains.

An early evening train took her to Cedarcliff, where she found McCoy's car waiting at the station.

"Why so suddenly attentive, old dear?" she inquired, slipping into the seat beside him. "I didn't say what train I'd arrive on."

"Consulted a timetable and decided this was the most likely, though I'd have met the next if you hadn't turned up now."

"Such longing for my society flatters me beyond words." She grinned at him teasingly. "Only trouble is, I suspect some dark motive behind it—either anxiety to impart something that's happened here, or an equally selfish desire to learn what I've discovered, if anything."

"Well, from the fact that you put in more than two days in Milton I guessed you'd dug up something Laney missed—naturally wanted to hear what it was," McCoy quite brazenly confessed.

"Alas! I knew it wasn't simply the wish to see me!" Tam's hurt tone failed to make the slightest impression; he knew her too well.

"Come on and tell me what you learned about Dunn before we reach the house."

"Sorry." She was suddenly serious. "What I heard in Milton isn't yet ready for publication, even to you. Besides, when you announced your intention of going after a certain copper-colored scalp, you and I officially parted company, if you remember. Not that I mean 'holding out on you,' once I'm sure of my facts—but at present they need a lot of verifying."

"So you mean keeping me in the dark until you've either built up another case or come 'round to accepting mine?"

"Practically, though I'll probably need your help before my 'case,' as you call it, is anything like complete."

"Humph! Maybe your pet red-head will be behind bars before then! So far I've found nothing to prove she and her lover didn't pull the job between them."

"Don't act hastily," she cautioned. "Perhaps in a week, or even less, I'll be able to offer you a different solution. By the way, have you spent any time over Bob Payne's alibi?"

"Why waste it when Lynn was murdered by a right-handed person and we know he's always been left-handed?"

"Doctors *have* been known to make a mistake," she argued. "Anyway I intend checking up his alibi, just to be sure."

In pursuit of that declared intention, Tam next day left the Trevor house as soon as luncheon was over. First she went to the village, did a little rather aimless shopping, ate more ice cream sodas than were good for her, and generally killed time until she saw Patience North on the main street. Even then Tam made no move, only kept Patience in sight until the latter went into one of the village dwellings, apparently to pay a call. Then Tam deserted the main street in short order, and, ten minutes later, knocked on the North front door. She had already ascertained that Jasper was absent on a short business trip, so Patience's visit in the village practically assured that the servant, Marta, would be alone; and it was Marta whom Tam had selected as the most vulnerable point of attack.

The neat, rosy-cheeked old countrywoman, who opened the door in response to Tam's knock, regretfully told her Mrs. North was out.

"Oh, I'm so sorry!" Tam sounded intensely disappointed. "I have so little free time and Mrs. North promised to show me her wonderful new ice-chest. I'm interested because I'd thought of buying one for a present."

"Indeed, and there's no reason why you shouldn't see it—though she does be out," hospitable Marta answered, quite as Tam had hoped she would.

The new ice-chest was accordingly inspected, and during the process the girl so exercised her winsome Irish charm that Marta begged her to accept a freshly brewed cup of tea.

"I'd love to, only you're in the midst of ironing. It's a shame to interrupt your work."

"There's no hurry, no hurry at all," Marta comfortably protested. "The missus has plenty of fresh underclothes in her bureau and even the kimono won't be needed tonight."

She busily started preparations for a generous tea, while Tam eyed the results of her interrupted labors, displayed on the wooden clothes-horse, with something approaching awe. Sheer silken undergarments, gauzy stockings, a negligee which deserved to be entitled a creation. Was it possible that these things actually belonged to Patience North? The thought of such costly fripperies under clothes such as she invariably wore was incongruous, to put it mildly— yet surely Marta could have no reason for describing them as hers unless she was telling the simple truth. Here Tam smiled quietly to herself; how often the search for some particular bit of evidence led to the acquiring of other, quite unforeseen clues, which either strengthened or destroyed the theory previously worked on.

In the interest of the chase she threw dietary caution to the winds and, despite the numerous ice cream sodas previously consumed, did such ample justice to Marta's homemade cake and jam that the good soul fairly beamed her flattered satisfaction. In response to Tam's praise of the rich quince preserve, Marta proudly told her that was "Mr. Bob's" favorite sweet, so introducing the name her visitor was interested in, without the need of any leading-up on her part.

"It must have been very painful for Mrs. North, having her brother suspected of the Trevor murder," Tam spoke with carefully gauged sympathy, just edged by curiosity. "How lucky that he happened to have spent the evening with her!"

"Wasn't it?" Marta agreed. "When Sheriff Dan Ferguson started asking questions, I was that frightened for Mr. Bob, that me heart up and sat in me mouth—him being sort of wild and hot tempered like, as long as ever I've known him."

"Surely you didn't think he could be guilty?" Tam dropped into her little pause.

"Not just 'think,' maybe. But there was the fear in me mind, seeing how he'd swore to get even with Mr. Lynn. Not a peaceful breath did I draw till Mrs. North told me it was her brother I'd heard talking in the living-room!"

"'Mrs. North told me.'" The phrase echoed surprisingly in Tam's brain; there had been nothing of hearsay in Marta's story as she, Tam, had hitherto heard it. She had understood that Marta unhesitatingly backed Patience's story of having spent the entire evening in the same room with her brother.

"Do tell me about what happened that night," she begged. "Of course I wasn't here then, but since coming to know all the Cedarcliff people I've grown so interested."

Nothing loath, Marta poured herself another cup of tea and, comfortably rocking, sipped it while she unsuspectingly recounted the events of that fatal July evening.

"You see, it was this way: Mr. North being away, we'd a light supper that night, and right after, Mrs. North started sewing on a dress she'd the wish to finish quickly. I cleaned up me kitchen and asked could I go to the sociable over to our church. Never being one to disoblige, the Mrs. made no objection and off I went, with leave to be out till eleven, or even later if I'd the wish."

"That left Mrs. North quite alone in the house?"

"All alone, yes, Miss; the master wasn't expected back till the Monday and this was of a Saturday."

"I see." Tam nodded. Marta sipped her tea with audible satisfaction, then went on:

"As bad luck had it, me head commenced aching and I couldn't no way enjoy the sociable, so home I come, along about ten or a speck earlier. Coming in the back way, quiet like, I heard the Mrs. talking in the living room, and a man answering her real soft and gentle—thinks I, now who can that be? The master never had such a kind sound in his voice and I was more used to hearing Mr. Bob a-laughing

and a-joking than I was to him speaking so soft. Mrs.
North, she heard me moving about and come out to the
kitchen saying would I fix a tray of cake and some iced
coffee, and while I did that same she found out why I'd
come home early and said I should go right to bed, she'd
lock up the house when she'd done sewing. But it wasn't
then she told me it was Mr. Bob she wanted the tray for."

"Didn't you think it queer, her not telling you who was
there?"

"Queer? Why would I, and him her own brother?"

"But you didn't know that at the time."

"I did not, but me head ached me too bad for thinking,
and when I'd got to me bed, it was too bad for sleeping
either. So I kind of heard voice and was able to tell the
sheriff as the visitor stayed real late."

"You didn't hear him leaving?"

"No, I must have dropped off, for next I knew the light
of the morning was peeking in me window and it was time
to get up."

"So you never really saw the visitor at all?" Tam wanted
to make certain of that point.

"I did not. But after Dan Ferguson started his questions, the Mrs. told me how her brother was here the whole
evening, so of course I answered him the same as she did."

"And when did Mr. North come home?"

"On the Monday, just like he'd said he would. It was
fishing he'd gone, up to the mountains, same as he often
done."

Having succeeded in shaking Bob Payne's alibi much
more effectually than she had dared to hope, Tam felt it
wise to depart before Patience's return. Of course the old
servant might repeat the whole conversation to her mistress, and was almost sure at least to mention the caller,
but that chance she had foreseen and discounted; destroy-
ing Bob's alibi was, for various reasons, worth the risk.

After a little more talk, she left the North house, but through the cemetery and reached the Trevor veranda just as tea was being served.

At Ivy's offer of a cup, poor Tam felt she never desired to see food or drink again.

"Please don't ask me! In the interests of justice I've devoured at least a gallon of ice cream, three different kinds of cake, oodles of jam and heaven only knows how much tea! I feel I'll never be able to look a tea cup in the face again."

"You sound positively tragic." Ivy laughed at her distressed tone. "What on earth have you been doing, and why the need of so much food?"

"The time hasn't come for explaining—but let's hope it's not far off! Do you happen to have seen Dips?"

"He was down at the barn with Bruno. I don't know if he's still there."

Tam proceeded to hunt him up and outline a plan which won his rapturous approval; above all things he loved midnight excursions, particularly illicit ones that might easily land them both in extremely hot water.

"Get a crowbar somewhere," she directed, on the point of leaving him. "I'll bring my own jimmy. On, and don't forget some putty and a little black paint. I'll meet you at one-thirty."

Back on the veranda she found Ivy had been joined by Linda and Mr. Trevor. The latter was looking much depressed. "There! I'm sure Nurse will prove an ally!" Linda gushed as she fluttered up to Tam and affectionately clutched her unresponsive arm. "I've been telling our darling invalid that the cure he really needs is a change of scene and climate; you agree with me, Nurse?"

"It all depends." Tam discreetly refused to meet her host's supplicating eyes; if the poor man hadn't pluck enough to escape from Linda's net, it was hardly her place to rescue him.

"Some lovely bracing spot, like Maine or Canada," Linda enthused, "where he can partly forget his troubles—we'd adore going along to help on the good work, wouldn't we, Ivy?"

The last suggestion was too much for her quarry. He muttered some indistinguishable excuse and fled indoors, leaving Ivy and Tam a prey to stifled mirth, and Linda distinctly offended.

All that evening McCoy, closely watching his young colleague, detected a suppressed excitement that set him wondering what particular devilment she was up to. But Tam skillfully evaded all attempts to corner her, and, pleading a headache in which the Inspector had not a particle of faith, retired early. He hung about until the hour grew so late, and his host so sleepy, that he was finally forced to depart unsatisfied and still nursing suspicions regarding Tam's activities. Had he waited another hour he might have seen her stealthily issuing from a side door, accompanied by Dips.

The night was ideally dark, its waxing moon hidden behind thick clouds, so that the two felt fairly secure against chance observation. Besides, the window they had selected for invasion was on the shadowed side of a house, away from the road. Crowbar and jimmy had been brought in case of need, but when possible Tam preferred more delicate implements. A glass cutter, skillfully handled, soon separated a small pane from its putty margin—Dips meanwhile holding a rubber suction-disk firmly against the glass to prevent its falling inward—and once the pane had been lifted out the window catch could easily be reached and unfastened.

The noiseless lifting of the sash required only a bit of patience, then Tam slipped in, leaving Dips on guard. First a desk in the large living-room absorbed her attention; it had been left unlocked and the finding of what she

wanted was only a matter of a little time. That first part
of her search completed, she stole softly along the hall to
a smaller room next the kitchen; there she carefully closed
the door, and, still venturing no other light than her torch,
investigated the contents of a glass-doored cupboard.

This second half of the quest yielded less definite results, but they contented her sufficiently to send her back
to the opened window and the waiting Dips. Once outside, Tam thrust a hand in through the aperture left by the
removed pane, and relocked the window; then, working at
top speed, she replaced the glass, using new putty mixed
with a little black paint to avoid leaving her work in a
condition to attract the householder's casual eye. Thereafter the two conspirators left the sleeping house as stealthily as they had approached it.

12
What a Woman Knew

"Feel like a confidential talk, Mac?" It was early the next afternoon when Tam calmly invaded the study where he was going over some papers.

"Depends on who does the confiding," was his cautious rejoinder, "you or me."

"Well, first of all I want to tell you about Ronald Dunn."

"Eh? So you dug up something important that got by Laney?"

Tam nodded emphatic assent. "Still, it wasn't altogether his fault. Being a woman, and favored by the little gods of luck, I hit on a source of information hardly accessible to him."

"You would! Go on and let's have it."

"To understand, you must realize that while Milton is close to Boston, it is really quite independent of that city and has an individual life of its own, very similar to that of any small town or village—its own shops and stores, more or less centering around a large chocolate mill. Now I've a pet theory that in such a place very little goes on unknown to the salesgirls in the local shops, so I spent my days making quite unnecessary purchases in all the Milton stores, energetically cultivating the salesgirls during the process.

"Given a reason for using it, and we Irish have a gift of the blarney. I made friends with nearly every woman who waited on me, and as trade lay under a blight of hot-weather dullness, they were all quite willing to gossip. The local papers had had long write-ups about Ronald Dunn and his unaccountable accident in Cedarcliff, so it was easy to bring the talk around to these articles and mention that I hailed from the village where their respected fellow citizen lay ill and probably dying. That set them off in good style; nearly everyone had some incident, personal or hearsay, to relate about the injured man.

"It wasn't until the third day, however, that I heard anything really helpful. Then an over-dressed, rather catty young woman began enlightening me as to just how deceitful Ronald Dunn really was.

"I gathered she'd had designs on the youth herself, and was soured because he failed to reciprocate; but that's a side issue and doesn't affect the value of what she told me.

"It seems, five or six years ago Dunn wasn't as wealthy as at present—he's inherited an uncle's fortune sometime during the last couple of years—and he lived in her mother's house as a paying guest. That's why the girl knew so much of his intimate history. Getting down to cases, she told me Dunn at that time worked for a prominent Milton lawyer whose wife was very popular and extremely beautiful. Said lawyer was too busy to care about accompanying his wife to all her social engagements, so she fell into the habit of using young Dunn as a convenient escort.

"Nobody seems to have especially remarked the fact, except for this one girl, my informant, whose eyes were sharpened by jealousy. She soon discovered that Dunn and his employer's wife were not only constantly together at social affairs, they were also, meeting secretly at a little inn. Of course the girl didn't admit it, but I think she actually spied on them and possibly warned the husband, though of that last I'm not sure.

"Anyway, he found out what was going on, and, I imagine, learned the thing went deeper than a mere flirtation. There was a frightful row at the inn. which was hushed up, because keeping it from general knowledge was to everybody's advantage, including the innkeeper's.

"A few weeks later the lawyer sold his house and disappeared, taking his wife with him. He gave out that he'd been offered a wonderful opportunity in California and meant taking advantage of it, so the sudden departure caused very little comment, though nobody seems to have ever heard of them since.

"So you see, old dear, you weren't far wrong in saying Dunn must have some secret sins up his sleeve."

"Humph! Interesting and casts a new light on his character," was McCoy's rather dissatisfied comment, "but darned if I see how it helps."

"You will," Tam promised. "I haven't told you the lawyer's name—and what's more, you won't get it just yet; there's another angle to clear up first."

"Think it's good work to hop about like a flea on a hot griddle?" he sarcastically inquired.

"Perfectly good, when there's a method in the hopping," she retorted. "Next we'll amble back to the morning Dips found the stranger at the foot of the cliff. Remember how the stretcher couldn't very well be taken down to the brook, so you men carried him up to the cemetery level?"

"Naturally. The poor devil came to as he was laid on the stretcher, and tried to grab his head—must have hurt like merry hell, I suppose."

"That wasn't the only time he came to," Tam reminded him. "As we neared the cemetery wall he opened his eyes and struggled to get up. Don't you remember?"

"Can't say I do," McCoy acknowledged after a little thought. "What does it matter, anyway; what's the idea?"

"Careless of you not to have paid more attention! It was what he muttered then, that sent me to Milton."

"Jumping Saint Peter! You're enough to turn a man's hair gray! Why don't you say what you're driving at?"

"Don't you even remember that he spoke?"

"Vaguely, now that you've forced me into thinking back. Something about 'strength,' wasn't it?"

"Word for word his speech was, 'Only give me strength— I'll wait—I *will* have patience—only give me strength!'" Tam repeated the words slowly, almost solemnly; McCoy nodded.

"Yes, that's it; needed strength to stand the pain, I suppose."

"Idiot!" Tam sounded thoroughly disgusted. "Strength was only an incidental word! The key lay in his sentence, 'I *will* have patience!' Doesn't that tell you anything at all?"

"Devil a thing."

"Not even when he says 'patience,' as we pronounce a personal name, not a verb?—And there's a woman of that very name in the immediate neighborhood?"

"Lord, Tam! You're not trying to rope Patience North into this case, are you?"

"Just that!" she snapped back. "Only take the trouble to repeat his words, substituting any woman's name you like in place of 'Patience,' and you'll see they bear quite a different meaning."

"I *will* have Ruth," McCoy slowly did as she requested. "Hu-m-m, does sound different, I'll admit."

"Of course it does—it suggests that, injured and suffering as he was, he still hadn't given up the purpose that brought him here, he still meant going after Patience if only he could get the necessary strength. At least, that's something of the meaning his words held for me, and they

set me thinking like mad. Then another small incident
happened that same morning that added fuel to my dawning suspicions. If you remember, when we left the Poole
house, bent on investigating the top of the cliff in search
of possible footprints, it was still early and news of the
accident hadn't had time to spread much. Yet when we
met Patience North, her first question showed she knew
all about it, and furthermore, she seemed distinctly disappointed when told that the stranger was still alive; she'd
heard he was killed outright, so she said. Right then I began wondering exactly how much she knew—and when we
found those footprints almost telling us some woman had
pushed Dunn off the cliff, I felt fairly certain she was the
woman!"

"Great Jehoshaphat, Tam—you're sure making a moun-
tain out of a molehill!" McCoy protested. "A delirious man
mutters a word that may, just conceivably, be a name; a
woman living close by hears about an accident sooner than
you think she's any right to— That's not enough to start
suspecting her, if you ask me."

"Still think so when I tell you the Milton lawyer's name
was North?"

"The one Dunn worked for?"

"Yes."

"But girl, don't you see it's not possible?" he wrathfully
demanded. "Jasper North couldn't live in two places at
once!"

"Who told you he was living here five or six years ago?"
Tam inquired with an irritating placidity. "Might be wiser
to spend a little more time asking questions about the
neighbors, a little less chasing ownerless wheelbarrows!"

"Trying to tell me the Norths haven't always lived in
Cedarcliff? Rot! They're always spoken of as natives."

"Jasper North was born and brought up here," she admitted, "but Patience wasn't. I've known that all along

and supposed you also knew it. After the Dunn episode set me thinking, I started making more intimate inquiries. There's no secret about the fact that Jasper North left the village ten or twelve years ago and only returned between five and six years later; then he came back, bringing his wife as she's known here. Still later, perhaps three years ago, Bob Payne appeared on the scene and through his brother-in-law's influence he was given a position in the Trevor bank—Jasper and Lynn had been boyhood friends and renewed their old intimacy as soon as Jasper returned from his long absence."

McCoy frowned, still unconvinced, then emitted an exultant chuckle. "Sounds great, Tam, wonderful; but you've clean forgotten what the lady looks like!"

"Oh, no, I've not! Simply discounting her present appearance."

"All I can say is, if you can picture young Dunn losing his head over her, you've got some imagination!"

"Her beauty does require a bit of taking on faith," Tam acknowledged. "But I believe that's her husband's fault."

"I'd be more apt to blame it on the Lord." McCoy was still chuckling. The notion of drab Patience North in a love affair evidently tickled his sense of the comic. But Tam refused to be either annoyed or turned aside from her chosen train of thought.

"He looks a dour, tyrannical sort of man. Isn't it possible that after her ramble along forbidden paths in Milton, he makes her hide her natural beauty so it sha'n't cause further trouble?"

"Never heard of such a thing!" McCoy's tone held pronounced skepticism.

"Neither did I, but that doesn't prove it couldn't be true. Besides, it's easier to believe than that the Patience we're accustomed to looking at could seriously have attracted North himself. Just remember, Jasper North's wife was known in Milton as a beauty; of course, he may possibly have rid himself of the first and got a new wife in the meantime, but would Patience as we know her have drawn him? That's highly improbable, moreover the time between his departure and his coming here was too short. Also that wouldn't account for Ronald Dunn's appearing on the scene."

"Well, even if you're right—which, mind you, I'm a long way from admitting—what's all this North family history got to do with Lynn Trevor's murder?"

For answer Tam drew a folded sheet of notepaper from her pocket and tossed it across the table.

"Ever seen that writing before?"

He opened it, closely scrutinizing the half-dozen lines it contained, dawning recognition in his eyes.

"Ye gods! It's the same writing as the love-note we found in Lynn's pocket! Where'd you get it?"

"From Mrs. North's desk!"

"When?"

"Last night."

"How?"

"That's something discretion advises keeping to myself," she informed him. "As a police officer you might think my methods a trifle high-handed; but so long as I wasn't caught—"

"Great Horn-spoons! I believe you raided the North house!" he accused. "Knew you were up to some devilment—so that's what you were planning!"

"I haven't said so."

"Not necessary, I know your ways—no conscience at all when you're nose to a murder-trail!"

"It doesn't matter how the letter was obtained," Tam argued. "Proof's what we need! Patience can't deny that's in her handwriting, or that the love-note found on the body exactly matches it."

"So—" McCoy fumbled for a cigar and slowly lighted it. Tam's revelations had left him slightly dizzy and all his ideas badly, needed readjustment. "It was Patience whom Lynn Trevor fell for, not Daphne!—But if that's true, why is the Poole kid acting suspiciously? What's she hiding?"

"That's a puzzle I mean trying to solve without further loss of time," she assured him, her firm, beautifully turned chin slightly out-thrust. "Likewise, why she was so interested in the mysterious stranger."

"If ever a murder case deserved the name of a love tangle, this is it!" McCoy spoke with an aggrieved air. "Love and jealousy motives are about all we've run up against since the investigation started. Then, with a sudden alert change of tone, "Hell! Patience can't be guilty! Her brother's alibi works both ways, for her as well as for him!"

"You mean it would, providing the alibi was worth anything," Tom amended. "Naturally the same point struck me, once I began thinking about Patience, so I took the trouble to ask a few questions and found the alibi only rests on Patience's unsupported word."

"Wrong! Everybody swears the maid Marta's above suspicion of complicity. And she testified Bob Payne spent the whole evening with his sister!"

"But neglected to add that her knowledge of the fact went no deeper than what Mrs. North had told her. Marta admits she didn't see the visitor, doesn't even know at what time he arrived or left."

"The devil you say! Positive?"

Tam nodded, then gave him a brief account of her stolen call on Marta and the latter's story as told under the mellowing influence of numerous cups of tea.

"Humph! Puts a different color on things," he remarked when she had finished. "Got any more evidence against her?"

"A little. While Clancy was in Milton, hunting up Dunn's record, I set Dips to privately investigating the

North house, or rather the grounds, stables, garage and
so forth. Way off in a corner where they're in the habit of
burning rubbish he found the remains of a bonfire, not
a recent one, but the accumulated rubbish left by a long
series. Digging about in the heap of ashes and half destroyed scraps, he found a partly burned knife-sheath and
a good-sized piece of the sole of a woman's shoe; you know
how slowly and incompletely leather burns unless subject-
ed to terrific heat. I sent both to a chemist for analysis—
the knife-sheath was too far gone to react satisfactorily
to his tests, but the shoe-sole yielded traces of tar!" She
smiled at him. "Still think I'm chasing a mare's nest?"

"Begins to look as if there might be some method in
your madness. Anything else?"

"Nothing conclusive. Acting on the theory that one of
her husband's knives might have been used for the murder
and afterward replaced so it shouldn't be missed, I went
through a cupboard next the kitchen that I'd seen while
visiting with Marta; a place where all his knives, fishing tackle and hunting stuff in general is kept. Sorry to
say there was no realistically blood-stained hunting knife
awaiting discovery; but I did find a short, wide-bladed
knife such as the doctors describe as responsible for the
death-wound, and it had quite recently been thoroughly
cleaned, even scoured—its blade was much brighter than
any of the other weapons."

"Clever, if she simply cleaned and replaced the knife
in its usual place, instead of getting rattled and trying to
hide or destroy it as they generally do." McCoy was evidently accepting the new suspect's probable guilt. "Think
she's the nerve to keep her head like that?"

"A woman clever enough to carry out the deception
regarding her looks that I believe she's been practicing
here, ought to be capable of rapid thinking when covering a murder, is at stake. Remember, whoever killed Lynn

Trevor had plenty of time to work out a subsequent plan of action." Here she caught sight of his horrified expression and barely suppressed a chuckle. "I know, you've just realized that if Patience is guilty, not Ivy, you automatically lose Rodney Poole as an accomplice— Don't worry, old dear, couldn't Ronald Dunn fill the role?"

"Providing he was in Cedarcliff at the time, but I've heard no whisper of any unknown man hanging about before, or directly after, Lynn's death—it was weeks later that the mysterious stranger turned up."

"That was an angle that bothered me while in Milton; discreet inquiries revealed that Dunn was in the Adirondacks on July 7th."

"Then he can't have helped Patience hide the body!" Disappointment rang loud in the inspector's tone.

"Not if he stayed there," she admitted. "Still, they're only a few hours away in a fast car. The thought struck me that Jasper North was also in the Adirondacks on the same date."

"You mean they may have met?"

"Not exactly," she hedged. "But suppose Dunn saw the older man, perhaps without being seen himself, and realized that since Jasper was enjoying a solitary holiday Patience must be alone; wouldn't he be apt to try and see his former sweetheart—that is, of course, if his devotion still retained any warmth?"

McCoy slapped an enthusiastic fist against the table. "Carry on a step further and we get the possibility that Dunn had clean lost track of the Norths! And seeing Jasper enabled him to pick up their address from some obliging guide or hotel man. Nothing more likely than that he'd hot-foot it down here, knowing his lady-love was all alone. Then, let's suppose he found she'd consoled herself with a new lover and was putting in the time of hubby's absence with Lynn— Phew!— We get a three way quarrel, and

either Patience or her former lover dealing the death blow
to Lynn—you can take your choice which!"

"I thought of something like that having happened!"
Tam's expression was almost suspiciously meek, but he was
much too excited by the new angle of the case to notice
her. He rushed on:

"Best thing is to face her with the love-note and what
we know about her past and try to force a confession. With
Bob Payne's alibi smashed, she'll have to own up who was
really with her, and long odds it was Lynn Trevor." Here
the recurrent thought of Patience's drab plainness obtrud-
ed itself, effectually clipping the soaring wings of his hope
of a speedy termination of the case. "But, hang it all, Tam,
I can't visualize that woman as the core of a love-triangle!
Her husband, maybe—some men just naturally stay fond
of a woman once they're married to her—but a young fellow like Dunn, and Lynn, the husband of a beauty like Ivy!
I can't see it!"

"Perhaps, if you'll consent to waiting one more day before making any move, I can open your eyes to Patience's
possibilities. I won't actually promise, but I'll do my best."

McCoy considered. Delayed action always went more
or less against the grain, and his present longing was to
openly accuse the new suspect and see what happened;
only the memory of her looks deterred him; they rendered
the losing of any man's self-control on her account so
incredible.

"I'll wait," he finally rather halfheartedly consented.
"And in the meantime send a man up to the Adirondacks
to do a little nosing about."

"No need. Dad's up there taking care of that end, and
he'll let us hear the instant he learns anything."

She rose, stretched lazily and smiled at him, a faintly
enigmatic shadow about her narrowed eyes. "Till tonight,

then—I'll try to show you our anything but lovely neighbor in quite a new aspect." Then, refusing to ease his curiosity by telling him what she planned, Tam departed on
business of her own.

She felt that Daphne Poole had been allowed to dance
evasively away from all definite issues quite long enough.
It was time for that young lady to be brought sternly to
book, and forced or cajoled into telling what she knew!
Bent on catching Daphne unaware, Tam crossed the now
familiar cemetery and instead of directly approaching the
front door, skirted the Poole house in quest of its young
mistress. The afternoon was too gorgeous for needless lin-
gering within doors and she felt sure a country-bred girl
like Daphne would be somewhere about the grounds.

Her reasoning proved accurate, for presently she heard
a clear high voice lifted in song, and following its guidance discovered Daphne prosaically gathering fresh vegetables for dinner.

"Let me help!" Tam offered. "I'm an expert at picking
just the proper-sized beans."

Informally working along opposite sides of the same
vegetable row brought the two into close proximity and
tended to lower the slight barrier which Tam had always
felt between herself and the Dresden-china girl. She suddenly determined on open attack.

"Miss Poole, you and I have always talked at cross-pur-
poses. Won't you lay aside your distrust and tell me what
it is you've been hiding?"

"Mercy! Why suspect me of concealing some dark secret? Don't I look innocent enough to disarm even a detective?"

"Oh, looks!" Tam gave utterance to a small, derisive
sniff. "What woman ever paid the slightest attention to
lamblike innocence, as worn by any other woman? It's only
men who judge by such outward signs, we look deeper

under the surface; just as I looked into Ivy Trevor's heart, or soul, whichever you like to call it, and felt certain she was guiltless of all connection with her husband's murder."

Daphne's small fingers stopped in the act of picking a bean, and her eyes flew to Tam's face. "Did you do that?"

"Even more, I persuaded Inspector McCoy to share my view."

"Then—" The girl's breath caught in something close to a nervous sob: "Then Ivy's in no danger?"

"Not the slightest," Tam assured her, still apparently absorbed in careful selection of the right-sized pods.

"But the inquest! She was almost accused then."

"Because she struggled so hard to hide her love for your brother that she naturally drew suspicions of worse things on herself! If she'd only been more frank in the beginning, heaps of trouble might have been saved."

"Heavens, you know all about that?" Daphne gasped.

"Of course."

"And still believe they—she is perfectly innocent?"

"I'm positive on that point."

Quite suddenly Daphne abandoned all pretense of interest in the vegetables and sinking back on her heels, burst into a torrent of tears. Instantly Tam slipped into the role of consoler and confidante, while the girl soaked first her own handkerchief and then Tam's, as she sobbed out the story of her terrible fear lest Ivy and the brother she adored might be guilty of Lynn Trevor's murder.

"I knew they loved each other, had known it for months—and I knew they were together the night before Lynn was supposed to have gone away—so when his body was found, I thought he'd discovered their love and they, or probably Rod, had killed him! Oh, I suffered agonies! And I never dared ask Rod a single question." She broke off to mop still streaming eyes, while the beginning of a smile carved a tiny dimple in the cheek free of Tam's comforting shoulder. "What a goose I've been!" came her half laughed, half sobbed comment. "Lying to you about Ivy's being jealous of me, so you wouldn't dream she was really otherwise interested—and later on refusing a sample of my handwriting for fear it would hurt Ivy's cause in some unguessed way— Oh, I've been all kinds of an idiot!"

She had by this time so far recovered her equanimity as to wring out both soaked handkerchiefs and spread them over a bean bush to dry, then resumed her vegetable picking with a single regretful comment:

"If I'd only trusted Rod more!"

"It would have been wiser; he naturally hadn't an idea you were suspecting him. As a matter of fact, you all three behaved rather like scared children. Why, even Mr. Trevor has been backing and sidling like an agitated crab, and I imagine all he's really discovered is that Ivy and your brother are in love."

Again Daphne's nimble fingers paused in their work as another aspect of the case occurred to her.

"But if they're entirely innocent, who on earth did kill Lynn?"

"That's an unanswered question up to now." There were limits to Tam's frankness. "Hadn't you yourself an alternative suspect?"

Daphne flung her a side glance out of yellow eyes that had borrowed an extra glint of gold from her recent tears.

"Only a certain half suspicious curiosity about Ronald Dunn—though of course, I didn't then know his name; he was simply the mysterious stranger."

"I've wondered what aroused your interest in him."

"It was due to my bad habit of night prowling," Daphne confessed. "Often I can't sleep well, particularly at the full of the moon, and when that happens I slip out of the house and wander round till I'm tired enough to sleep soundly. Just by chance I ran almost into the stranger's arms one night near the church, and a few nights later I saw the same man steal into the shadows behind the North house. Seeing him twice like that, so close to Patience's home, set me guessing, and I remembered the face she'd claimed to see looking in at my window; could that man and this night prowler be the same, and if so had he any connection with Patience? It was in the hope of finding out something definite about them that I was sneaking around the church the night you caught me."

"How did you know he would put in an appearance that particular night?"

"I didn't. I'd been prowling about every night for a week and just happened to come so close to catching him, or perhaps them— Personally, I believe he and Patience were talking, and he jumped out the window when he saw or heard me, so as to distract attention from the building long enough for her to get away."

"Had you definitely connected the stranger's visits with Patience North?" Tam asked, anxious to know if the girl had arrived at the same conclusion as herself.

"Yes, though I'm afraid I can't give you any real reason, except Patience's fright when a strange face appeared at the window. It was more, I think, that I've always sensed something odd about Patience; you haven't seen her enough to notice, and besides you don't ramble over the countryside as I do. But just catch Patience away from her home and the village, sometime when she believes herself unobserved, and you'll find she's quite a different woman—she drops that plodding, clumpy walk and moves with the swift grace of a wild thing! Oh, I can't describe the difference, but it's a very actual one, just the same."

Tam nodded. "I think I understand."

"You *would!* Understanding seems to be your specialty, Nurse." But there was only frankness in the equivocal little speech, not a trace of malice.

13

The Real Patience

"Anything else as you'd like, sir?"

"No, Marta, nothing else."

"Then I'll bid you goodnight, sir." Before she had reached the door Jasper North glanced up from his book.

"Where's my wife?"

"Gone to her bed, being tired with a long day's sewing."

"Very well, good night."

When the woman had gone he ignored the tray of food she had placed at his elbow and returned to his reading. Either the book lacked interest or his thoughts were more absorbing, for after a little he ceased turning the pages, letting his eyes stare blankly into space.

For a while complete silence reigned in the softly lamp-lit room, then the door behind Jasper opened and a transformed Patience slipped noiselessly into the room. Her hair, usually straggling across brow and cheeks in lank disorder, was now freshly washed and fluffed in soft waves around a face no longer sallow and muddy-skinned, but clear as a flower petal; colorless lips were changed to an enticing scarlet bow, and brilliant blue eyes opened wide under lids no longer drooped to hide their beauty. Even the figure, relieved of its badly cut, clumsily fitting clothes, showed full sweeping curves, barely hidden under the orange and blue of her exotic negligee, while slender white

feet, thrust into heelless blue mules, shared in the general
transfiguration. She was beautiful, with the clinging, passionate beauty of a woman born not for man's comfort and
easement, but for his undoing.

"Jasper!"

At sound of his whispered name the man turned to
stare at her with icy disapproval.

"Will you never tire of play-acting?" His voice rang
harsh, almost threatening. "Is your beauty so dear to you
that even considerations of safety can't induce you to keep
it hidden?"

"Only for you, Jasper." She had stolen, soft-footed,
nearer to him when the lamp light played over her volup-
tuous, thinly covered body; but he remained as unmoved
as some image of wood, only the shadow of a sick distaste
lay like a blight across his rugged features.

"Can't you realize the danger is not yet passed? Only let
a villager, or even Marta, see you as you are now, and such
a blaze of curiosity would be lighted that in the end they'd
find out your responsibility for his death."

"Don't, Jasper! Please don't!" Her voice throbbed with
husky under-notes of fear and longing. "You give me nothing, no help or kindness—how can I bear my thoughts
alone?"

"Since when have your sins weighed so heavy? In Milton you told me only fools bemoaned accomplished facts."

"That was different—sins of unfaith, they're so tran-
sient, something that may enter the life of any beautiful
woman— But death—that's so hideously final!"

"Right!" he acknowledged grimly. "Either physical
death or the death of a man's long-suffering love!"

"Don't speak so," she pleaded, white hands hovering as
though they longed but dared not touch him. "Not now,
when I've come to love only you!"

"Love!" The word was a sharp, strident bark. "Much you know of love! Passion, of that you're a past mistress, I'll grant—but the gentler, deeper emotion that leads a man or woman, smiling, through any hell of suffering— What do you know of that?"

For answer she dropped in a fragrant silken heap, clinging arms about his knees. "Only try me, Jasper! Test this new love of mine in any way you like—you'll find it yours, utterly yours!"

For an instant the man seemed to weaken; a ray of softness flickered into his hard eyes, but it was gone almost as quickly as it had come. With a rasping sound his chair was pushed back so that he could tear free of her encircling arms and gain his feet.

"Too late!" His voice was a hoarse croak. "Once I would have died, gladly, to win your sole devotion—now Lynn Trevor's blood lies between us! Go!"

She seemed to realize that it was hopeless. Slowly she rose and crept, crushed and beaten, from the room, with Jasper, with one agonized groan, dropped back into his chair, face buried and powerful shoulders shaken by the silent sobs of a strong man under torture.

Outside the partly open window Tam touched McCoy's arm. Then, with no word spoken, they stole quietly away.

Only when the highway was reached did the Inspector give vent to his feelings in a long-drawn whistle.

"Some dame!" A handkerchief mopped his heated brow. "To think that seething volcano is walking round under the Patience North I'm used to looking at! How'd you know she meant staging that love scene tonight?"

"Mostly guesswork. Marta had that negligee you saw ready for pressing when I interrupted her work yesterday, and she told me it wouldn't be needed last night. She'd previously said that Mr. North was returning from

Beauty that was meant for man's undoing, not his comfort! "Will you never cease your play-acting?" his voice rang high, threatening

his business trip today; so I reasoned that the blue-and-orange creation was probably to be donned for his reception; a woman always likes looking her best when a man returns from even a short absence, and as such a garment had hardly fitted the Patience we'd hitherto seen, I thought she'd temporarily lay aside her plainness in its honor."

"Sure takes a woman detective to follow the quirks of the feminine mind!" McCoy spoke resignedly. "No man would have figured like that."

Tam only smiled wisely. "What is it Kipling says about the Colonel's Lady and Judy O'Grady, being sisters under the skin? We can read between each other's lines more easily than you men, that's all. But getting back to business—do you still think Patience is too plain to make any man lose his head?"

"Jumping Saint Peter! As she was tonight, I'd bank on her setting the whole Stock Exchange by the ears," he declared. "Pity to put such a woman behind bars."

"And you have the colossal nerve to accuse me of being influenced by feminine beauty," Tam jeered. "How about yourself?"

"Well, I suppose her looks wouldn't hit so hard if you were used to them; it's the damned contrast that does the trick. How the hell does she do it?"

"Make-up," was Tam's laconic explanation.

"But in broad daylight," he demurred; "I've seen her in the sun and never noticed anything odd."

"Partly because she was so plain you never really looked at her; nobody did. I remember what a shock it gave me when I saw her eyes were a wonderful pansy-blue. I even went so far as to realize that her features were good in themselves, it was the muddy skin and stringy untidy hair that repelled at the first glance and kept people from examining her closely—and then, her clothes! They were enough to hide the beauty of a Venus."

"Cleverest make-up ever I saw. She ought to go on the stage."

"I imagine that's where she learned the art—it's too consummate not to be the result of skilled training. An amateur would almost certainly have overdone it and made herself ridiculous. But, Patience succeeded in striking exactly the right note; no lavish use of actual make-up, just a too-dark powder that made her skin look sallow and the rest mostly a carefully studied effect of neglected hair and atrocious clothes."

"Well, I suppose how she hides her attractions is neither here nor there in face of the fact that Jasper practically accused her of killing Lynn and she didn't deny it! Wasn't a word out of her when he said her love came too late—Trevor's blood lay between them! Not court evidence, of course, but once she's arrested we'll get more, and what with her love-note and the rest, there is enough to start on. I'll swear out a warrant in the morning."

It was too dark for him to mark his young colleague's satisfied, but slightly remorseful expression. They had stopped just inside the Trevors' gate, for despite the late hour the house was still brightly lighted. Now, the question of Patience's arrest settled, Tam moved on up the path, the Inspector following. They found Rodney Poole with Ivy and Mr. Trevor in the living-room.

"Had to come over and tell you the news," Poole explained, catching sight of them. "Ronald Dunn is conscious, though partly delirious still, or at, least his brain's none too steady—he's mistaken Daphne for Patience North, and keeps begging her to elope, also goes over and over the scene of Lynn's entombment in the oak tree—they seem to have managed it together, he and Patience! At first I was all at sea, then his ramblings told me he'd been her lover and that Lynn had cut him out—looks as if they killed him between them, though he hasn't mentioned that part."

"Patience!" The startled exclamation came from. Ivy Evidently the last item had not been previously mentioned. "Do you mean she was the woman Lynn loved?"

"You knew he loved somebody?" the Inspector instantly demanded.

"No—" She hesitated, fugitive eyes on Rodney's. "Only, when a man grows so very indifferent to a wife who hasn't altogether lost her looks, there's usually some other woman in the background. But I certainly never suspected Patience; I credited him with better taste."

Here McCoy surprised and rather shocked them by emitting an hilarious chuckle. "Don't go condemning his taste till you've seen the real Patience," he advised. "Wonder to me is, how Trevor happened to see under the surface in the first place? Let's hope that question gets cleared up tomorrow, along with a lot of others."

Next morning the Inspector's hand was strengthened by a code telegram from Rance O'Brien which, when deciphered, told them that young Dunn had actually seen Jasper North from a distance on the morning of July seventh—had let this be known to the guide who was with him, and had even bribed the guide to obtain North's address from the lakeside hotel where he was stopping. As to whether or not North had seen his wife's former admirer, O'Brien had so far been unable to learn, but the chances seemed against it as Dunn had left the mountains almost immediately after his brief glimpse of the, lawyer.

"Dr. Poole thinks Dunn is pretty well out of danger," McCoy remarked when the message from Tam's father had been thoroughly digested. "With any luck we ought to pin the crime on the two of them—though I've a fancy it was Patience who struck the actual blow."

"Going to arrest her?" Tam asked, without committing herself to an opinion.

"Yes, I've the warrant in my pocket; want to come along?"

"Surely, and do you mind if I bring Dips? I've a really special reason for wanting him."

"He's too young to be in at the death—but if you want him I suppose you'll insist on your own way."

They collected Dips, who appeared to be waiting for them, then crossed the highway to the North house.

Her mistress was in, so Marta informed them, opening the door to the very room in which they had witnessed Patience's strange scene with her husband, less than twelve hours before. It was the everyday Patience who rose to greet them; gone all trace of her overnight beauty.

"You wished to see me?" She favored Marta with a far from amiable glance, but that good soul failed to catch it and departed, quite unconscious of having committed any indiscretion in permitting her mistress no choice in the matter of receiving her early visitors.

"Yes." McCoy drew out a legal looking document. "Sorry, Mrs. North, but it's my painful duty to arrest you on the charge of murder."

"Murder!" One hand went to her throat in the almost universal gesture of startled womanhood, the other flew out as if to fend away some hideous approach. "Murder!"

"The murder of Lynn Trevor, the man to whom you sent a love-note making tryst for practically the very hour at which he met his death!"

"I wrote no such letter!" Patience breathlessly denied. "Why should I? Lynn Trevor was nothing to me!"

"No more than your other lover, Ronald Dunn, I suppose," McCoy sneered.

"Dunn?"

"Oh; it's no good repeating every word I say—nothing to be gained by stalling, for we know the history of your life in Milton—know how your husband discovered your affair with young Dunn and tore you away, making you return with him to his native village, where you've posed as a plain, unattractive woman little likely to set any hearts afire. That was your husband's doing. Eh?"

Instead of answering, Patience only stared at him out of terror-widened eyes. "What else do you know?"

"Plenty!" McCoy nodded with exaggerated confidence. "That your accomplice insisted on haunting the vicinity, for instance, trying to persuade you into eloping, until your patience gave out and you pushed him over the cliff-edge."

"Oh my God!" Her terrified moan told him he was hitting close to the truth.

"A little softer skull and you'd have permanently silenced him—as it is, he's recovering and able to talk!" As he paused to let the threat of Dunn's possible confession sink in, Tam spoke for the first time since their entry.

"Don't forget the burned knife-sheath, Mac, and the hunting-knife that's been so carefully scoured!"

Patience whirled to face the newer enemy, something of desperation in the eyes that met and locked with Tam's; for a long moment it seemed to McCoy that the two held some intimate communion from which he was shut out, then, very suddenly, Patience threw herself into a chair, both hands covering her face.

"It's true," she whispered. "I'm guilty!"

McCoy gave vent to a triumphant snort. She had surrendered much more quickly and easily than he had dared to hope.

"It's my duty to state that anything you say may be used as evidence against you," he uttered the stereotyped warning, notebook already in hand. "But since you've confessed to the main charge, it can't do much harm to answer a few questions. Going back to the time when you lived in Milton—Ronald Dunn was your accepted lover?"

"Yes."

"It was on his account that your husband gave up his law practice there and came back to Cedarcliff?"

"His, and others."

McCoy's ears pricked at her words. "'Others?' What'd you mean by that?"

"Only that Ronald wasn't the first lover Jasper had found out about." She spoke with a dead indifference that seemed to relegate all lovers in general to the ranks of common incidents of normal life. "I was very unlucky, or perhaps careless—Jasper always discovered my little indiscretions. Not that there were so many," she added in a tone of impartial fairness. "Not more than three or four; and Ronald was much the most serious of them all."

She stopped, letting her head sink against the chair-back, a look of blank indifference spreading over her face. The Inspector eyed her with bewildered uncertainty—she was not behaving in the least as experience had taught him to expect anyone accused of murder to behave. Tears, defiance, sullenness he could have cheerfully met and coped with, but her passive indifference left him at a loss.

"He, your husband, made you conceal your natural beauty?"

"Yes. He said it had caused enough heartaches, he'd keep it from making any more."

"Original sort of idea. How'd he come to think of it?"

"I was on the stage before we married and the first role he ever saw me play was a Cinderella type—a homely little kitchen slavey in the first act—later a dancing butterfly. That dual role suggested how easily my good looks could be hidden by bad dressing and make-up—he forced me into resurrecting my old technique and using it."

"Must have had a strong whip-hand to make any woman do that."

"Oh, he had." Patience shivered slightly. "Though I enjoyed the deception in a way, it appealed to my love of intrigue, especially after Lynn discovered the truth."

"How'd he come to do that?" McCoy inquired curiously.

"An intensely hot day—a cool lonely lake, and my inveterate love of swimming. Lynn arrived on the scene unheralded and— Well, the secret was out."

"So—" After last night he could vividly imagine the vision that must have greeted Lynn Trevor's astounded eyes. "So that was how it began. And your husband never suspected?"

"No. He thought I no longer needed watching; my plainness acted as a safeguard."

"You'd neither seen nor heard from Ronald Dunn during the years you'd lived here?"

"No; I wasn't allowed to keep in touch with any Milton friends. I supposed he'd forgotten all about me."

"Until he unexpectedly turned up and caught you with a new lover?" McCoy prompted. For the fraction of a second Patience hesitated, then:

"Since I've admitted that I killed Lynn, why so many questions?"

"Want to make certain in what degree Dunn's implicated."

"But—but he had nothing to do with it!" She seemed horrified by the suggestion. "Lynn brought about his own death—when he learned he wasn't my first lover, he turned on me in a way no woman could tolerate—remember, I loved him or at least thought I did—I couldn't endure his insults, and the knife was there, close to my hand!"

"He was killed here, in this house?"

"In this room." She shuddered.

"And Dunn afterward helped you to conceal the body?"

"Yes."

"Was the idea yours, or his?"

"Mine, of course! How could a stranger know of the tree surgery being done by the Government experts?"

"How'd you happen to know the tar in that particular tree was still soft?"

"Because I had passed the men at work on it just before they stopped work for the day. After I'd killed Lynn—"

"She lies!"

The two chill words dropped unemphatically across her sentence, cutting it in mid-air, and Jasper North vaulted in through the open window with an agility amazing in one of his years and habitual dignity.

"It was I who killed Lynn Trevor."

14
Dumb Nemesis

"No! No!" Patience rushed to him, flinging both arms about his neck. "Don't believe him—he's only trying to shield me!"

"Hush." He stolidly unwound the clinging arms, imprisoning both her fluttering hands in one of his. "Marta overheard enough to realize what was happening and came to the office to warn me."

"I thought she'd do that." Tam spoke as McCoy stared dazedly from one self-confessed criminal to the other, uncertain where the guilt actually lay. "Arresting Patience seemed the only way to force a confession."

Jasper North turned to her; piercing eyes the only living thing in his dead gray face.

"I sensed you as my most dangerous enemy. How long have you suspected the truth?"

"Only recently—" She was interrupted by an indignant explosion from McCoy.

"Mean to say you've been using me as a catspaw; Tam O'Brien? Lying about Mrs. North's guilt?"

"On the contrary, I never once said I thought she was guilty—only pointed out certain events which might have occurred."

"Aiming at making her husband confess?"

"Exactly. Try as I would, I couldn't find enough evidence to lend any hope of conviction—but I felt he'd speak rather than let Patience suffer in his stead. You, as a police officer, could scarcely arrest her unless you believed in her guilt, your professional conscience wouldn't let you, so I had to deceive you just a bit."

"But Ronald Dunn; you bracketed him as an accomplice!"

"Oh no, I only suggested the possibility—you jumped at the idea and filled out the details for yourself, overlooking the fact that no stranger could have killed Lynn Trevor."

"Why not?"

"Paddy."

"By the Devil's hoof, I'd clean lost sight of that dog!" The Inspector's anger yielded to self-reproach.

"So I noticed," Tam smiled at him with just a hint of apology. "I was horribly afraid you'd recall how Bruno described Paddy's reception of the man he saw prowling around the house the night of the murder. Once you remembered the dog greeted him as a friend, I knew you'd realize Dunn couldn't have been that man; there was no possibility of his being known to Paddy, for he'd never been near Cedarcliff at that time. Besides, whoever poisoned the dog must almost certainly have lived close by—that's one of the things that led me into wrongly suspecting Ivy and Rodney Poole." She turned to directly address Jasper North. "What made you realize that Paddy's dumb testimony might prove dangerous?"

He stared at her uncertainly, then apparently decided on entire frankness.

"I was at the station when you arrived and recognized you, as I'd watched you at a recent trial where your testimony practically clinched the State's case against the accused. When Mr. Trevor met you, I guessed you'd been engaged to investigate Lynn's disappearance, and I felt sure you'd prove less blind to the significance of Paddy's actions than the rest had been. As it happened, I possessed some arsenic originally bought as rat poison, so I wrapped some in a slice of meat and fed it to the dog, who know me too well to feel any lasting distrust. My mistake was in not having attended to him sooner, but one hardly expects to be overtaken by a four-footed Nemesis."

"That's aptly put," Tam conceded. "If Paddy hadn't tried to scratch away the tar concealing his master's body, and thereby collected enough on his paws to track around the Trevor house, we might never have discovered the contents of that hollow tree—alone, the trail of the red ants wouldn't have enlightened us. Did you realize the dog know what had been done?"

"Partially. There's no point in further concealment—I'd like to tell you both exactly what happened. Not with any idea of self-justification, but merely to unburden my mind."

Here McCoy's professional conscience forced him into delivering a warning.

"You're not obliged to admit anything; the onus of proof rests with the State."

"As a lawyer, I'm aware of that," North nodded. "But since I intend admitting my guilt, it hardly matters."

He cleared his throat us if troubled by an unwanted dryness, and tit a look from Tam, Dips, who had skipped out of the room and returned a few moments previously with a gloss of ice-water, promptly offered it to North, standing close to him while he drank it.

"Thanks." He handed Dips the empty glass. "My wife won't like what I say; but the time's come for plain speaking, and she can't deny the truth of my words. By nature, I believe myself to be as honorable and straight dealing as the average man, but I've always been cursed with a fiendish temper, the sort that makes one see red under sufficient provocation. And my wife never failed to supply plenty of the latter. Almost from the day of our marriage I realized she possessed a wanton's heart." At Patience's protesting little moan, he only glanced at her with chill rebuke. "She was incapable of real devotion to any one man—adulation and the first tempestuous stages of courtship were as the breath of life to her; a taste her stage career had probably done much to foster. Unfortunately for me, I gave her an absorbing love; the spell of her beauty and charm held me in a net from which I was unable to extricate myself, even the discovery that she was unfaithful failed to free me, and when she swore reformation and future constancy, I was fool enough to believe her.

"The same thing happened again, and still again, and while I'd lost all belief in her promises, all faith in her honesty, my love refused to die. Such weak idiocy brought its own reward. Patience continued to dance gayly along her chosen path of intrigue, until finally even my long-suffering devotion rebelled. Ronald Dunn was as decent a lad as ever walked; when she deliberately enticed him into loving her, my patience snapped; I brought her away from Milton and compelled her to hide the beauty which had proved so fatal to my happiness and to the peace of other men.

"You'll wonder why I didn't divorce her. I couldn't; mingled pride and the shreds of my love forbade it. Here in my old home I've found the nearest approach to contentment that's come to me since our marriage. With her beauty hidden, I was no longer compelled to watch Patience exerting her siren's charm, and I was actually fool enough to believe that at last she was solely mine. I should have known that such women never change, they merely learn more effectual modes of deception."

Overcome by the bitterness of his own thoughts, North lapsed into a short silence, during which none of the others moved; only the buzzing of a fly against the window and the soft sound of Patience's piteous weeping stirred the heavy stillness. Then he lifted a face that seemed to grow momentarily more aged, and went deliberately on:

"During the week ending July seventh, I took a long-planned holiday in the Adirondacks. It had been arranged that Patience should accompany me, but she backed out at the last minute and I was too sunk in my new, hard-earned security to suspect the reason. I left Cedarcliff on the Friday, and on Saturday morning was casting in a favorite stream when one of the guides, a man who happened to be under certain obligations to me, sought me out to inform me that a stranger whose name he didn't know had seen me earlier that morning—himself unseen by me—and had later bribed one of the other guides into obtaining my address for him. As soon as he had it, this unknown stranger had his car brought around, asked directions concerning the best roads going toward New York City, and left apparently in a tremendous hurry.

"At first the incident made little impression, but it had shadowed my enjoyment of the fishing, and the more I thought of it, the more my curiosity was roused. Finally I went back to the hotel, where a few inquiries gave me a glance at the register; at sight of Dunn's name ugly suspicion poked up its head. I more than half guessed the truth—guessed that the unexpected sight of me had stirred in him a hope of regaining touch with Patience—the fact that he so carefully had avoided an encounter with me proved it was renewed acquaintance with my wife, not with me, that appealed to him.

"I felt sure that, possessed of my address, he would go direct to Cedarcliff, and, uncertain as to how Patience might receive him, but led by past experience into fearing the worst, I determined to follow him. As it happened, Dunn was delayed by engine trouble; I overtook and passed his stalled car, but he failed to recognize me behind dark driving-glasses and a pulled-down cap. I'd been late in starting, so didn't reach Cedarcliff till eleven that night.

Some instinct of caution led me into stopping my car some distance down the road and approaching the house on foot. The place was in darkness, save for a low light in this room; by this time, my suspicions were fully aflame. I stole softly around to that window and peered in through a crack left by a carelessly pulled blind. It was as I had feared.

"Patience lay in the arms of a man whose face I couldn't see—I supposed him to be Dunn, who, I imagined, must have passed me while I stopped for dinner. The one glimpse was enough to remove all doubt as to the nature of his reception!

"I left the window, entered through a side door to which I always carried a key, and stalked in on the astonished lovers. At Patience's alarmed cry the man sprang up and turned to confront me— It was Lynn Trevor!

"Up to that instant I'd been more disgusted than actually enraged. But realization of my double betrayal drove me mad, I think. Lynn Trevor was my closest friend, a man I'd loved and trusted since boyhood. Patience had almost taught me, during these last years of my fancied security, to believe in her single love for me—and all the time they'd been joining hands in deceiving her fool of a husband! The temper I'd learned to control but never had killed drew a red veil before my eyes and without conscious purpose I caught the hunting-knife from my belt and attacked him.

"We struggled, but I was the stronger and I suppose my rush took him more or less by surprise. The end was measured in seconds and when the furious blood receded from my brain, the hunting-knife was deep in his heart. No need to describe my remorse—I'd killed him because of a woman who wasn't worth the taking of any life, and from that instant I hated her as fervently as I had hitherto loved her.

By some perverse alchemy of her twisted nature, the very act that finally ended my infatuation kindled hers—from the moment that I'd proved my strength, as she calls it—"

He paused with a bitter sneer. "From that moment she has felt for me a devouring emotion which she dignifies by the name of love. It made her persuade me, against my better judgment, into concealing my crime and afterwards disposing of Lynn's body in such a way that we hoped it might never be discovered.

"Such hopes, as you know, were dashed by my innocent dumb Nemesis."

All through the long confession, McCoy had been rapidly filling the pages of his plump notebook, now he looked up, pencil still poised.

"Was Paddy here with his master when you arrived?"

"No. He come on us in the cemetery as I was wrapping the newspapers around Lynn's body. He tried to defend the body against my touch."

"Wonder you didn't silence the dog then, once for all."

"As a matter of fact, I thought I had," North acknowledged. "I struck him over the head with a stone, meaning to kill him but actually only stunning him, as it turned out. I'd no time to learn whether he was dead, for his barking, as he tried to drive us away from Lynn's body, had drawn another witness. Young Dunn, driving down the road in search of Patience's home, had seen our cavalcade in the distance as it crossed the highway. It was a bright moonlight night, and while he didn't recognize either of us, Lynn's body slumped in the wheelbarrow made him suspect something wrong—he heard Paddy's frantic barking and, following it, discovered us at work over the body! Right there the poor boy proved the strength of his devotion to my wife—he gave in to her pleading and left us to carry on, promising to keep his mouth closed. As far as I know, he's kept that promise."

"I'd like to question Mrs. North as to that." McCoy turned to her. "Didn't young Dunn haunt the vicinity in the hope of seeing you?"

"Yes." She nodded a weary assent. "And he succeeded. After seeing him look in at Daphne's window, I tried to avoid meeting him, but failed. He begged me to elope with him, but of course I couldn't, I no longer cared for him. As you know, it finally ended in my pushing him off the cliff, though the act wasn't altogether intentional; he insisted on pleading his love and trying to kiss me, and— well, he fell. Jasper won't understand, won't acknowledge that all my sins were largely his fault— He was always too self-controlled, too fond of his own dignity, to give me any outward demonstration of more than a restrained, temperate sort of affection which never stilled the craving I was born with, for love, love and still more love! I never believed that any real fire lay under his surface calm. When he proved it existed, by killing a man for my sake—I—well, I gave him a passionate devotion which he's been scornfully rejecting ever since the night Lynn Trevor died!"

"I've heard of such things." North regarded her with an impersonal curiosity. "But I never believed that murder could actually endear a man to any woman."

"Only when it's committed for love of her—through jealousy—" Patience eagerly tried to explain, but his cold voice cut her short.

"The subject fails to interest us. I think the Inspector and Miss O'Brien would rather hear the conclusion of that night's work." Then speaking, more to Tam than to the others, he went on:

"When Dunn had left us, we succeeded in removing the tar and getting the body to stand upright inside the hollow tree. But the stuff was too hard to replace with anything like convincing smoothness. While we lighted the workmen's fire, intending to remelt the tar into workable shape, Patience was visited by an inspiration. Why not try to steal into Lynn's room, and by packing and removing one of his bags, give the impression that he'd gone away of his own accord? You see, he'd told her of that afternoon's quarrel with his wife.

"I decided on at least attempting to carry out her scheme while the tar was reheating, and congratulated myself that Paddy wasn't about to give the alarm; then, glancing toward the spot where I'd last seen him, I found the dog was gone. Patience told me she'd seen him rise and stagger away while Dunn was with us. I suppose my blow must have dazed him so that, recovering consciousness, he forgot what immediately preceded it, and like all animals when hurt, simply made for home. Evidently he recovered enough to hear and resent my visit to the house, but he proved amenable enough when I spoke his name and ordered him to hush—you see, he regarded me as an old, tried friend, known since his puppyhood, and probably thought I'd struck him accidentally. Still, his earlier experience must have put some caution into his canine brain, for when I went back to the cemetery after packing the deceptive bag he must have followed me without my knowledge. By the time I returned, Patience had filled the lower part of the hollow tree with tar, but the upper portion of Lynn's body was still free of it, so that I was able to replace his keys, one of which I'd used to open his private drawer, in the pocket where they belonged."

"What were you after, among his papers?"

"Some letters from my wife, which she told me he kept there. I found and afterwards destroyed them, but hadn't time to restore the papers to order because I heard voices approaching and realized that Ivy must be returning from wherever she'd been. I stepped out through the side window only a few seconds before she opened the sleeping-porch

door. Why she failed to see the light burning in the bedroom before I heard her coming and put it out, has always
puzzled me."

"Probably too much interested in her companion. Besides, the jog of the house and the thick foliage would
pretty well cut it off from anyone approaching by way of
the lane."

"At any rate, her sudden arrival gave me a most un-
pleasant turn. Perhaps that's why I failed to see Paddy
following me. I never imagined that he might constitute a
real danger until several days later, when Mr. Trevor told
me how peculiarly the dog was acting; then I went to examine the oak tree, and found it marked by Paddy's nails
where he'd evidently tried to disentomb his master's body.
As I'm fond of dogs, and no one seemed to read the meaning of his behavior, I neglected silencing the dumb witness
against me until the arrival of the famous Tam o' Shanter
caused me a shock of apprehension. Even then I bungled
the job and gave Paddy too small a dose!"

"On the contrary, he would have surely died if Dr.
Poole hadn't taken him in hand so quickly," Tam declared.
"I'm glad you failed! Paddy's a love of a dog, to whom I
owe an immense debt of gratitude, and besides his death
then wouldn't have saved you-—the tracking home of the
softened tar was the real cause of your undoing. Without
it we might never have found Lynn's body, but once that
happened, and we suspected a murder'd been committed,
the rest was only a question of time and hard work. For,
again using Paddy's previous testimony, we knew the murderer was someone the dog considered as a friend. By a
process of elimination we were bound, sooner or later, to
discover which one, among those he knew, was guilty."

"Suppose someone else, your brother-in-law, for instance, had been actually accused of the murder—would
you have kept silent?" asked McCoy.

"I doubt it. In fact, all along I've been tempted to confess and end the suspense. It was Patience who persuaded me into letting her establish an alibi for Bob, instead of clearing him by the truth."

"Surely, at the inquest, you must have observed that some suspicion pointed toward Ivy Trevor?" The last question was Tam's and after a moment he answered it:

"Knowing her innocence, I thought she'd have no difficulty in proving it. Of course, I didn't know she possessed another guilty secret she was determined to hide at any cost." He laughed harshly. "Nice moral community, weren't we? Daphne Poole and I seem to have been the only ones not indulging in illicit romances!"

"Still, if you didn't intend implicating Mrs. Trevor, why put the stained wheelbarrow in her tool-shed?" Tam persisted.

"Why so sure that I did?"

"I wasn't certain until ten minutes ago. When we closely examined the barrow—after learning it was a trespasser in the Trevor tool-shed—Inspector McCoy and I found the tiny silver plate which is usually inserted in the better sort of pocketknife, caught in a crack in the boards. The plate was bare of initials, but he let me keep it in the hope that I might find the knife to which it belonged. I failed until today; now I know the plate fits your jack-knife."

North's fingers went hurriedly into a coat pocket, only to reappear, empty.

"Kindly explain what you meant."

"My small assistant was once a professional pickpocket. I sometimes find his skill in that line very useful and today brought him along with instructions to get your pocketknife for purposes of comparison; you see, I wasn't then sure if we'd be able to force you into confession. While you drank the ice-water he so opportunely offered, he dipped into your pocket and extracted the knife, then carried it to the window and standing with his back to the room, tested it to see if the tiny plate found in the wheelbarrow fitted; he promptly signaled me that it did."

"Good! Lord, I never felt the boy touch me!"

"Naturally not—one never does with a professional pickpocket."

"Hardly imagined I'd left a clue like that lying around loose! While I noticed the plate was gone from my knife I felt no uneasiness—I must have forgotten I'd used it in cutting the papers into convenient strips for wrapping about Lynn's head and shoulders."

"That was another thing which convinced me he'd been entombed by some former friend," Tam remarked. "A stranger wouldn't have been so squeamish about protecting his body from the hot tar. But you haven't yet told us why you put the wheelbarrow in a neighbor's tool-shed."

"Merely because it was the easiest place to reach. I took the thing home from the cemetery without realizing it was blood-stained, a fact I discovered when the stable light struck it. It would have been wiser to wait until next day and then burn it, as I did burn my knife-sheath because of the blood-stains left when I stupidly replaced the knife in the sheath after drawing it from Lynn's breast."

"Why were Mrs. North's shoes also burned?"

"You apparently didn't need my confession—you'd built up a strong case without it! As to the shoes, they were badly stained by the tar she'd carelessly stepped into."

"Funny thing, we never could trace that wheelbarrow," McCoy grumbled. "I spent hours over the infernal thing."

"Not so remarkable. I found the barrow in a corner when I came back to Cedarcliff. It must have been left by one of the tenants who rented the house during my long absence, and had probably been on the place so long that none of the tradespeople remembered selling it; in fact it may even have been brought here from some distant place by the tenant who finally abandoned it. The only person who'd be at all likely to recognize it was an old gardener who'd done occasional work on the place, and there was no certainty even of that. After I'd had time to think everything over, I did plan to retrieve the barrow and burn it, but no convenient opportunity offered and I neglected to make one. There's more than a grain of truth in the old saying that even the most careful criminal always overlooks some detail." He rose slowly to his feet and without a glance toward Patience, went a few steps closer to Inspector McCoy. "Since I've answered every conceivable question, why not end this gruesome interview and take me into legal custody?"

"I've no warrant for your arrest, but if you're willing to waive that formality and come along—"

"Surely! There's nothing to be gained by delay."

"There's just one more question I'd like to ask you, though strictly speaking it's nothing to do with the case," McCoy still lingered. "Experience having taught me just a little about women, I'd like to know how the devil you forced a beautiful woman into posing as an ugly one."

For answer North flung a half pitying, half derisive glance toward his weeping wife.

"Well, having tried every other method known to man, I resorted to the oldest of them all, physical force. I beat her into submission!"

"Jasper North, of all people! Even now I find it hard to believe!"

It was some hours later, and Tam had been elucidating events up to date for the benefit of Ivy and her father-in-law.

"Personally, I find it much more difficult to place any faith in your account of Patience North's hidden beauty." Mr. Trevor spoke with open skepticism.

"You'll almost certainly have reason to alter that opinion at the trial," Tam predicted.

"IVY!"

They heard the call and the sound of running feet, before Rodney Poole dashed into sight and leaped up the steps.

"I've just heard Jasper North's confessed!"

Without a spoken word Ivy went to him, both her delicate hands extended to his eager clasp. For a long moment they stood silently looking into one another's eyes, then, still silently, went down the broad steps and across the lawn, his arm protectingly about her.

"It's an ill wind that blows no good—" Trevor cleared a throat grown suddenly husky. "They intend marrying, after a decent interval, and I, for one, believe they'll be very happy."

"It was because you'd discovered their love that you wanted me to drop the case, wasn't it?"

"Yes, my dear. I was shocked, but— After all, she deserves a more honest love than any Lynn gave her. Love, my dear, is a very wonderful thing. Life's rather barren without some touch of it." He sighed resignedly. "I shall probably end by grasping the best imitation within my reach and—marry Linda!"

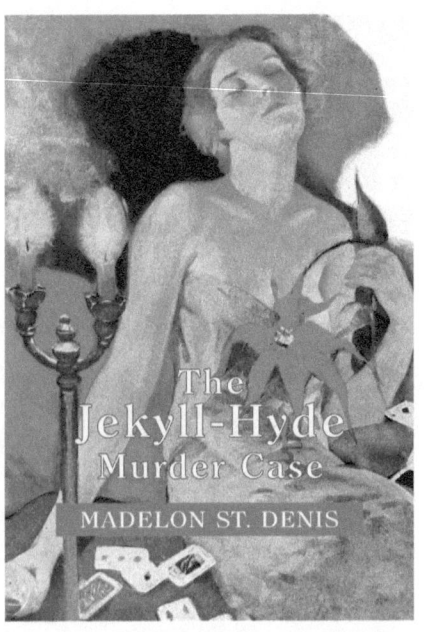

Coachwhip Publications

CoachwhipBooks.com

Coachwhip Publications

CoachwhipBooks.com

I'll Hate Myself in the Morning

Murder on the Left Bank

Elliot Paul

THE BAND PLAYED
MURDER
EDITH HOWIE

CRY MURDER
EDITH HOWIE

NO FACE TO
MURDER
EDITH HOWIE

Coachwhip Publications
CoachwhipBooks.com

WHISPER
MURDER!

VERA KELSEY

FEAR
CAME
FIRST

VERA KELSEY

LATE
for the
FUNERAL

Douglas and Dorothy
Stapleton

The Railroad
Murder Case

R. M. LAURENSON

Coachwhip Publications
CoachwhipBooks.com

MURDER IN THE FAMILY

NICE PEOPLE MURDER

Mary Hastings Bradley

NICE PEOPLE POISON

MURDER IN ROOM 700

Mary Hastings Bradley

MEDORA FIELD

WHO KILLED AUNT MAGGIE?

BLOOD ON HER SHOE

MEDORA FIELD

Coachwhip Publications

CoachwhipBooks.com

MURDER
À LA RICHELIEU
THE ADELAIDE ADAMS MYSTERIES
ANITA BLACKMON

**THERE IS
NO RETURN**
THE ADELAIDE ADAMS MYSTERIES
ANITA BLACKMON

THE CRIME,
THE PLACE,
AND THE GIRL

DOUGLAS AND
DOROTHY STAPLETON

CRIME IN
CORN-WEATHER

MARY MEIGS ATWATER

Coachwhip Publications
CoachwhipBooks.com

Coachwhip Publications
CoachwhipBooks.com